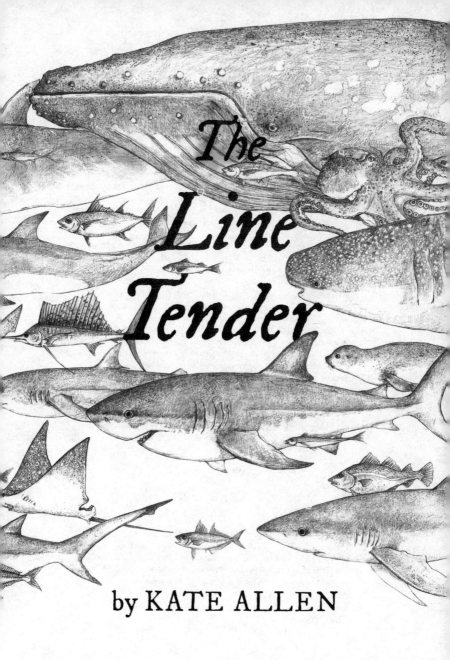

The Line Tender

by KATE ALLEN

PUFFIN BOOKS

PUFFIN BOOKS
An imprint of Penguin Random House LLC, New York

First published in the United States of America by Dutton Children's Books,
an imprint of Penguin Random House LLC, 2019
Published by Puffin Books, an imprint of Penguin Random House LLC, 2020

Visit us online at penguinrandomhouse.com

THE LIBRARY OF CONGRESS HAS CATALOGED THE DUTTON EDITION AS FOLLOWS:
Names: Allen, Kate, 1977- author.
Title: The line tender / by Kate Allen.
Description: New York, NY : Dutton Books for Young Readers, [2019] |
Summary: "Following a tragedy that further alters the course of her life, twelve-year-old
Lucy Everhart decides to continue the shark research her marine biologist mother left
unfinished when she died years earlier"—Provided by publisher.
Identifiers: LCCN 2018017872 | ISBN 9780735231603 (hardcover) |
ISBN 9780735231627 (epub)
Subjects: | CYAC: Sharks—Fiction. | Friendship—Fiction. | Single-parent families—Fiction. |
Loss (Psychology)—Fiction. | Grief—Fiction. |
Family life—Massachusetts—Rockport—Fiction. | Rockport (Mass.)—Fiction.
Classification: LCC PZ7.1.A439 Lin 2019 | DDC [Fic]—dc23
LC record available at https://lccn.loc.gov/2018017872

Puffin Books ISBN 9780735231610

Design by Jessica Jenkins
Text set in Sabon

Printed in the United States of America

5 7 9 10 8 6 4

For my parents,
Pat Allen and Cliff Allen

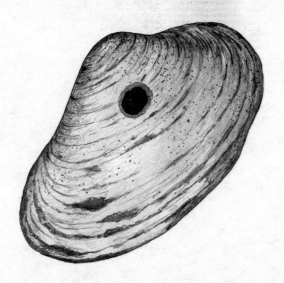

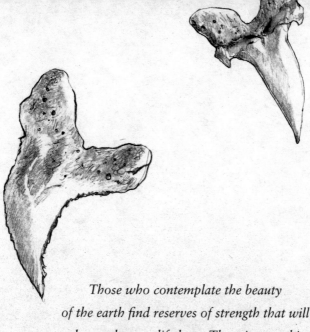

*Those who contemplate the beauty
of the earth find reserves of strength that will
endure as long as life lasts. There is something
infinitely healing in the repeated refrains of
nature—the assurance that dawn comes after
night, and spring after winter.*

—Rachel Carson

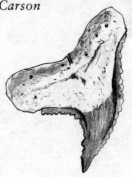

1. *Shark*

THE MORNING THE GREAT WHITE CAME TO ROCKPORT, my best friend and I were sticking our fingers into the coin returns of every pay phone in town. We averaged about two dollars a day during the summer. Most days we cashed in for candy.

"Seventy-five, eighty, eighty-five," I chanted, sliding the nickels around in his palm. "We have a buck forty-five."

Fred shrugged and gestured with his head toward the store that sold gummies and penny candy.

Sometimes I wondered if almost thirteen was too old to be cleaning out pay phones for candy, but no one was watching us and it was hard to turn down free money. We headed over to the Country Store and, like magicians, turned quarters and dimes into gelatin-based sweets.

I pushed open the door to the shop, walking into an incense-and-candy fog. Fred immediately went for the candy section. He knew what I liked, so I let him pick. I wandered over to the postcard rack. As I spun it around, it squealed like a rusty playground swing. I scanned the column of familiar photos of Rockport, Motif #1 and Twin Lights, winding my red ponytail into a spiral with my finger.

It was dark and cool in the shop, with the low wood

beams and the painted floorboards. An older man dropped a coin into the player piano, which pushed out a quick song like the kind from a carousel.

Fred dropped a plastic sack of gummies onto the glass countertop beside the register and I walked over to see what he had chosen. He'd gone with a familiar mix, heavy on worms and frogs.

Mrs. Lloyd weighed the bag. The beaded chain holding her reading glasses glittered like a ruby necklace.

"Zero point three-three pounds," Fred guessed.

The window on the digital scale read 0.34.

"Not your day," she said, smiling at Fred.

As Mrs. Lloyd pulled the bag of candy off the scale, the jangly bell rang over the shop door and stopped abruptly as the door slammed against the inside wall. A boy I'd never seen before came running in.

"Easy," said Mrs. Lloyd, tracking the boy with her eyes.

"Hey!" the boy cried, his flip-flops smacking against the creaky wood floors. He ran to another kid whose arm was elbow deep in a barrel of fruity Tootsie Rolls—a candy neither Fred nor I bothered with. Face-to-face, the boy put his hands on the other boy's shoulders. I assumed they were brothers, same thick, dark hair and identical molasses-brown eyes.

"HUGE SHARK!"

The hard *k* sound bounced off the ceiling. I watched the boys and waited for the rest of the story.

"What?" Little Brother's eyes were as wide as peanut butter cups.

Fred walked over to the boys. "Where?"

"At the wharf! A fisherman dragged it in," said Big Brother.

The boy was spitting like crazy. He looked like a fifth grader. From his excitement, I would have guessed it was a megalodon. He was wearing a Rockport T-shirt, which meant they weren't local, and they sounded like they were from the Midwest. I figured any shark was huge to them.

"Where are you from?" I asked them.

"Ohio," said Big Brother.

"You ever seen a shark before?" I asked.

"Only at an aquarium." His eyes were still wide.

I looked at Fred.

"Let's go," he said, snatching the gummies.

"Go where?" I asked.

"Shark. C'mon," he said, taking off into the bright sunlight.

He left the door wide-open, and I knew there would be a lecture from Mrs. Lloyd about air-conditioning costs, so I pulled the door shut behind me as I followed him out.

"Okay, but we're not staying out there all day," I yelled ahead. We had plans to watch a movie at Fred's house.

Fred looked back over his shoulder for a second, though he never stopped jogging. I kept my eye on him and took my time, passing the Chinese import shop in the row of storefronts on the bottom floors of shingled houses, the ice cream shop covered in ivy, and telephone pole after telephone pole with a tangle of slack wires.

It was hot. July hot. The last thing I wanted to do was hang around the wharf in zero shade. I didn't care what the fishermen had dragged up.

I made the turn onto Dock Square, past the candy store with the taffy pull in the window, and then the asphalt turned to granite slabs as I made my way onto T Wharf. It was the spot in town where fishermen unloaded the catch. A crowd of people at the edge of the harbor blocked my view. I looked for Fred.

The smell was strong—not Gloucester Harbor strong, but fishy. It wasn't just the herring for the traps or the catch itself. There was an earthy smell that came from the algae-green wood and the water that stood still inside the breakwall.

I spotted Fred and followed him as he wove his way through the people. It made me anxious and reminded me of trying to keep up with my dad at the Fourth of July parade. I struggled to stay close to Fred, following in his path. I heard his voice before I saw the shark for myself.

"Whoa," said Fred.

I moved beside Fred, budging my way into the front row to see the shark's body being pulled by the hoist from just below the dock. As the mouth came closer, my eyes went straight to the huge, serrated teeth, gnarly and sticking out at different angles. Rows and rows of white barbs poking out of the shredded gums, pink like strawberry taffy. My instinct was to move away, but I couldn't help walking toward it until we were nearly face-to-face. I imagined that my whole body could fit inside, as if I were sliding into a sleeping bag, the jaws opening around my hips.

"Is that a great white?" I asked.

"I'm pretty sure," said Fred. He pulled out his inhaler and took a puff.

After his second puff, he said, "Your mom would know."

I nodded. My mother would have known.

2. *The Expert*

MY MOM WAS A BIOLOGIST AND THE RESIDENT SHARK expert for Massachusetts. When I was a kid, though, I mostly thought she smelled like fish. No matter how hard she scrubbed, when I hugged her, the smell was always there. When I was older, I asked Dad how that had been possible. He said the scent came from dissecting sharks and whales, from cutting away layers of blubber and plunging her hands inside the cavities of marine creatures that were twenty times her size. He said that if she wasn't up to her elbows in the guts of a newly dead animal, she was in the ocean, looking for live ones—salt and microorganisms flowing through her hair. Even if she hadn't been near the water in days, we could still smell those fish oils in her skin. There was no doubt that she would have been called to the dock for this shark.

Fred took another puff on the inhaler and looked at me. "Are you okay?" he said. "Your face is red."

"Just hot," I said.

A few men pulled the shark up higher by ropes and pulleys, and I followed the length of the shark's white belly from nose to tail. It was probably as long as three fishermen stacked end to end, though it twisted as it was raised above the crowd, tied in three places.

It was not like one of those great photos from the early 1900s where a crazy-looking guy posed with a good-looking mako hung from tail to nose in a straight line. This shark was so large that it had to hang over the water, away from the dock. Its body bent into a horseshoe. The rope near the mouth bound the shark like a rubber band around a fat wrist, separating the head from the rest of the body. The shark looked a little ridiculous at first, but the menace was inescapable if you kept looking.

"We've seen it," I said to Fred, staring at the shark. "Can we go?"

"You know what this means?" he asked. Not that it mattered whether I knew or not, because he was going to tell me anyway.

"What?" I asked.

"The field guide!" he said with wide eyes, like a strawberry-shaped, wobbly goldfish.

The field guide was an extra-credit project for science class that was due in September. Signing up for it was Fred's idea, and I agreed to help, knowing I'd probably need a little cushion in case I bombed a test during the year. Fred did the writing. All I had to do was provide the illustrations, and I could draw as well as Fred could explain taxonomy.

There was one rule about the field guide: We had to see the specimen with our own eyes to include it. So far, we'd come across a black-capped chickadee in Pigeon Cove and a spotted salamander in a rainwater pond in the woods.

That was about the best we could do on land, until we were staring at the great white shark.

While Fred's brain went straight to the field guide, I couldn't shake my mom. I imagined her on the dock, between us and the shark, sizing it up before figuring out how she was going to lay it out on the ground.

"What are they gonna do with it?" Fred asked.

"Good question," I said.

Laughing, the fishermen in orange waders emerged onto the wharf from the docks below. I knew one of their laughs right away.

"It's Sookie," I said, taking a deep breath.

Sookie was a fourth-generation Rockport fisherman and he was a good friend of my parents', except he hadn't come by the house in a long time. Still, standing on the dock, he looked like the same man I'd known my whole life. He wore mirrored sunglasses and his brown hair was sun-bleached. Sookie had a reddish tan, not a golden tan like the kind the beachgoers had. He was sweating twice as much as I was.

Lester, Sookie's deckhand, was at Sookie's side in matching orange pants. He was seventeen and hung out with Fred's older sisters.

A crowd of other fishermen and spectators circled around them, and I knew from the handshakes and back slapping that Sookie had caught the shark.

"Why would he want to catch a white shark?" Fred asked.

"I bet it was an accident," I said.

I broke away from the crowd and walked into the mob of people surrounding Sookie.

"Sookie!" I yelled.

His head turned toward my direction. He patted someone's back and moved to the edge of the mob where I stood. Fred was right behind me. Sookie pushed his sunglasses onto the top of his head. His eyes were wild.

"Lucy! What do you think?" he said, pointing to the shark.

"It's enormous," I said. "What happened?"

"We were fishing for cod and it got stuck in the net."

I winced. "Yikes."

"What do you mean, 'yikes'?" he said. "It's a huge fish."

"Well, it's kinda useless now, right?" I asked.

"Yeah, what are you going to do with it?" Fred asked.

"I thought we'd let it hang for a few days. Keep the tourists off the beach," said Sookie.

"You really should think about calling a biologist," Fred said.

Sookie hesitated for just a moment. "Lucy's mom was the only one I knew," he said. "I would've called her from the boat."

Sookie looked at Fred first and then at me. He pulled my ponytail gently with his fishy hand. I looked him in the eye. I always liked hearing someone else remember my mom.

"Sook!" yelled another fisherman, holding up a camera.

"Gotta go," he said.

I looked at Fred. "Are you ready to go *now*?" I asked.

"There's your dad," he said, pointing.

He was still in his work clothes. Dad was a detective, so he didn't wear a normal police uniform. He looked like a regular guy in khakis and button-down shirt. His hairline was wet with sweat. His Minolta SLR hung from a strap around his neck. He'd probably been on his way somewhere else too. I yelled to him three times, but my voice was absorbed into the horde. He settled on a spot in the mob and looked up at the shark, dangling above the crowd, as he raised the camera to his face. I read his lips: "Sweet Jesus," he said, as he smiled like a kid.

3. *Scuba Diver*

AFTER POSING FOR OUR PICTURE WITH THE SHARK, FRED and I rode our bikes slowly in the street beside Dad. We climbed up the big hill in the center of town. The sidewalks were clogged. Everyone was excited about the huge, dead shark hanging at the wharf, but all I wanted was a cool shower and something to drink.

To my right, we passed the bookstore and art galleries. Gaps between the buildings revealed alleyways that led right to the ocean. The flashes of blue on our walk were subliminal reminders of the sea that circled the shops and houses in town.

"Dad, what if you saw the great white in the water when you were diving?" I asked. "What would go through your head?"

"A great white? *Panic*."

"What was it doing off Rockport?" I asked him.

"Looking for food, I guess."

"Isn't it too cold for them?"

"No. Great whites swim as far north as the Gulf of Maine," he said.

"Will there be more?" I asked. I knew the answer. I'd heard it from my mom and from Fred.

Dad shook the loose change in his pockets, the way he did when his brain was elsewhere.

"Dad?"

"I'm sorry. What?"

"Will there be more sharks?" I repeated, slightly annoyed.

"Sure. Where there are seals, there are whites." He must have sensed the storm brewing in my stomach because he added, "But they're still rare up here."

I slapped every parking meter with my palm, as we biked past Front Beach.

"When I was a kid, if you brought a seal's nose to the police station, the clerk paid you fifty cents. Fifty cents a seal," Dad said.

I gasped. "Why?"

"Because they attracted sharks, and people thought they made a loud mess of the harbor."

"That's terrible," I said.

"Yes," he said.

"Did you ever kill a seal?" I asked, knowing the answer was *no*.

"What do you think?" he said.

"I told Sookie he should call a biologist," Fred said. "I don't think he's gonna do it."

Dad was quiet for a moment, and he gave the change in his pockets another shake. "Sookie's a stubborn guy. He only hears what he wants to hear," Dad said. "I bet somebody's already on the way."

Fred looked sad or angry, I couldn't decide which.

"Tom, could you talk to Sookie?" Fred asked.

"Me?" Dad said. "I don't think that would have any effect."

"When was the last time you saw him?" I asked.

"A while ago," he said in a crabby tone that suggested we were done with questions.

"Are you okay?" I asked.

"I'm fine," he said. "Just hot."

We passed the little houses beyond the beach and turned onto King Street, then onto Smith. We coasted past our neighbors' houses, dumped our bikes in my driveway, left Dad behind. We went into my house, took turns in the bathroom, and I poured a couple of glasses of water. Fred didn't appear to be in any hurry to go home, so we went back outside and sat on the front stoop.

"Sox play Detroit tonight," Fred said.

I nodded.

"Maybe we can watch after dinner?"

"Sure," I said.

"I want to enter the shark into the field guide," he said. "Do you think it will still be there tomorrow?"

"I bet it'll be," I said, though I had no idea. I wanted to reassure Fred, but I also didn't want to go back to the wharf today. "Does my dad seem *off* to you?" I asked.

Fred shrugged. "A little. He doesn't like crowds."

I shook my head. "I don't think that's it."

I was about to suggest we head down to the wharf in the morning when I noticed my dad in my peripheral vision, naked in the side yard.

"Oh God," I whispered.

Dad pulled his scuba suit off the clothesline and worked his feet through the ankle holes, pulling the black rubber skin up his legs like he was yanking on pantyhose, his backside to Mr. Patterson's house. It was horrifying. There was Mr. Patterson on the porch, motionless in his rocking chair, police radio chirping beside him.

"Dad," I said, with my face in my hands.

"What?" he said, with his suit now covering his lower half like he was dipped to the waist in tar. "I'm going to head down to Back Beach for a bit before dinner."

"You're going in the water?" I asked.

"Yeah." He was oblivious.

Fred translated for me. "She means because of Sookie's shark."

"Lucy, that shark was caught twenty miles off Rockport. And do you know what the chances are of being attacked?"

"Yes. One in, like, millions."

"That's right."

"He'll be okay," Fred said. "But I wouldn't do it. Not at dusk."

My dad rolled his eyes, gathered up his gear to drive a couple of blocks to the beach. While the wheels of his old

Volvo wagon spit gravel down Smith Street, I wondered what would happen if Dad saw a great white while diving off Cape Ann. Because of the plankton and the cold, green waters, he might only be able to see twenty feet in front of him on an average day. If an eighteen-foot great white came into view, it would already be *on* him. If, for some chance, the shark swam out of sight, there would be no way of knowing how close it remained. It would be difficult for my dad to spot the position of his buoy in the murky water, and great whites attack their prey from beneath. I had to shake off the thought.

I turned to Fred. My gut was churning. "Do you think that's weird? I haven't seen *your* dad naked before—*anywhere*."

"Yeah, but he doesn't *live* here anymore."

"You think I should apologize to Mr. Patterson?"

"Only if *you're* naked."

"How hard would it be for him to put his suit on in the house, or wear a bathing suit underneath?"

"Not hard."

I picked at my rubber sole. Fred searched his pocket for his inhaler and took a puff.

"You okay?" I asked, swiping my hand across his back.

"Oh, crap," he said, still sucking in. "There's my mom." He put the inhaler back into his pocket. "I'll call you later," he said.

Maggie waved at me from her front steps and then she walked over. Maggie Kelly was tiny, but she walked with the thunder of a rhino. Even though she was a single mom with three kids, she still managed to keep an eye on me too.

"Your face is red, Freddy. Have you been using your inhaler?"

"Yes, Mom," he said. "I'll see you later."

"Bye," I said, smiling up at Fred.

Maggie escorted Fred into their house across the narrow street.

After he left, I looked at my sneakers for a moment before calling out, "Hi, Mr. Patterson."

"Hello, Lucy." The old man waved like the pope. "Your father has a hairy keister."

"Yes, he does."

"I don't like looking at it."

"No, sir."

4. *Empty House*

DAD SPENT MORE TIME UNDERWATER THAN HE SPENT ON land. He was a scuba diver, both professionally and recreationally. If he wasn't hauling people out of the water (dead or alive) with the rest of the Salem Police dive team, he was hunting our lobster dinner off the coastline near our house. It was typical for Dad to receive a call from the dive team outside his regular hours at the police station. Salem Police divers did double duty, working regular shifts as uniformed police officers or detectives, but also responding to emergency situations. It seemed like there had been more calls than usual that summer—people driving off bridges or swimming in dangerous waters. I didn't like it when he was gone. When he was at the bottom of some harbor, the house felt empty. But he was always moving like a shark, swimming in order to breathe.

That night, I learned later, some moron had driven his truck into Salem Harbor and that Dad was called to the accident scene to help fish him out. There was a mostly thawed block of chicken on the countertop that Dad might have cooked had he stayed home that evening. I didn't know the first thing about transforming raw meat into dinner, so I sat at the kitchen table and leaned over a copy of the *Silver Palate Good Times Cookbook*. Some of the recipes had my mom's notes in the margin. It was always strange to see her handwriting, to see something that was so distinctly hers and that was still here.

"Check at twenty-five minutes!" she wrote.

"Can substitute with olive oil," in another place.

She had been gone five years. Most of the time, Dad and I were okay without Mom, even though I still thought about her every day. But my grief for her was like a circle. I always came around to missing her again. It could be a birthday that triggered the new cycle or something more unexpected, like finding something in a drawer that belonged to her.

I started reading the recipe names in a whisper. "This one sounds simple. 'Whole Chicken Baked in Salt. Lemon and ginger cooked in the cavity perfumes the bird.'"

But the recipe called for four pounds of Kosher salt. *Four pounds.* I wondered how a chicken cooked in four pounds of salt was still edible. When I reached the part where the chicken cooks for two hours in a wok, I closed the book. We didn't have a wok. Or four pounds of salt.

I opened the fridge. The combination of old food and *nothing* made me lonely. I pulled out the garbage can from under the sink and started pitching—lettuce, both rusted and soggy; fourteen-day-old moo shu pork that looked deceptively edible; and peaches with skin like a mummy's. There was half a Corningware dish of lasagna from last weekend. I imagined bacterial colonies beginning to creep up, so I used a knife to wiggle it out of the pan and let it flop into the garbage, which had just about reached its limit.

I wiped the shelves with a wet rag. Now we were left with nothing—a half gallon of milk, a pitcher of Tang, some onions, and a door full of stuff in jars. I poured a glass of the orange drink, grabbed a short stack of stale saltines from the pantry, and walked into the den. *I gotta learn how to cook.*

Through the open window I could hear the leaves rustling in frequent swirls of wind and Mr. Patterson listening to dueling radios on his porch—the Red Sox on WEEI and a police scanner. It was an odd and familiar sound—Joe Castiglione's voice and the crack of the bat, layered with occasional farty blips and cryptic messages between cops and dispatchers. I didn't hear anything from the dive team.

Eventually I walked over to the TV and flipped it on, taking a leisurely stroll through the channels on my way to the Sox game. And there was Sookie on Channel 7, wearing his mirrored sunglasses and speaking into the reporter's microphone. I never saw people I knew on TV. I picked up the phone.

"Turn on Channel Seven. Sookie's on TV."

"Okay," Fred said.

I could see the wharf and the harbor behind Sookie.

"Holy crap, it's T Wharf."

"I'm getting there, I'm getting there," he said.

The camera panned to show the shark's body in the near distance, hanging awkwardly from the winch. The shark would have looked powerful swimming in the ocean, but it seemed freakish hanging in a loop on the dock, bunched up in some places and stretched out in others. The reporter asked Sookie if he had ever seen a great white in all of his years of fishing off the Massachusetts coast, and Sookie said, "Nope. Only in the movies."

"There we are!" Fred yelled. "Over by the garbage cans."

I didn't like seeing myself on TV. I looked way too tall, especially standing next to Fred. The reporter looked into the camera and launched into a brief history of great white sharks in the North Atlantic. Fred was getting agitated. I could hear him breathing into the receiver.

"That's *wrong*," he said. "They can swim in subarctic water."

Then the news story cut to a section of old footage.

And there she was. Talking to the camera while sitting on a boat, her hair blowing around, her face with freckles like mine.

"Lucy. That's your mom," Fred said.

"I know," I said. Somewhere off camera, a man asked her a question.

"Am I afraid? Being in the water with sharks?" She grinned. "No. You just have to remember that you are swimming in their home. You have to know how to behave when you are the guest."

"Seriously," Fred said.

"What would you like people to know about sharks?" asked the man off camera.

She looked up at the sky for a moment. "I guess that there is so much we *don't* know about them—where they go, or how many there are. And we fear what we don't know. If we knew more about sharks, maybe we would be in a better position to help ensure their survival."

The boat kept rocking and my mother smiled at the camera. It was as though she were smiling at me. At me. I looked right into her eyes and it was like we were staring at each other. The fine lines around the outer corners of her eyes deepened as her smile grew. I shuddered. The phone slid from under my chin and hit the floor.

I didn't take my eyes off her.

She sighed and kept looking at me. Then, too abruptly, the clip ended and we were suddenly back on T Wharf with Sookie and the newscaster. It took me a minute to realize that I had been talking to Fred. I wiped my face, bent down, and picked up the receiver.

"Lucy?" said Fred.

"Fred, what was that?" I asked, sniffling.

"It was a clip from an interview with your mom."

"No, I know that. But where did it come from?"

"I don't know. Ask your dad."

"He's not here."

"Are you okay?"

"Not really."

"Want me to come over?" he said.

"I don't know," I said. "I'll call you back."

The circle had begun again.

5. *The Storm*

I HUNG UP THE PHONE AND TURNED OFF THE TV, MY SCALP tingling like the static inside the blackened television. I felt as restless as the wind picking up in the trees. Seeing her on the screen was like being with her in a dream and wanting the dream to last for hours. I wondered where the interview had come from and if there was more footage. I wished I could remember her words exactly.

I looked at a photo on the bookshelf and picked it up, holding it close. It was probably taken moments before a dissection. Mom was wearing white coveralls, like a painter, and a headlamp glowed like a star in the center of her forehead. In the dark, she knelt beside a giant shark that had spilled out of the ocean and beached itself in the sand. The shark's teeth were as white as her miner's light.

Her face was four feet away from the shark's open jaws and her expression was completely calm, as if she were posing for a family photo with Dad and me. This made sense, seeing that the shark was dead and, therefore, unable to raise its head and snap her in half. It was a safe time for collecting data. But that was the thing about my mom. She would have collected data four feet away from a *live* shark.

There was something shiny in her pocket. I moved the

photo closer to my face like an old lady reading a menu. The object looked like a silver pen, clipped to her pocket cuff. I wondered if it was a roller ball or a ballpoint (roller balls were smoother to draw with) and I wondered how she could use a pen if her hands were covered in fish guts. I wondered what she wrote and if she made sketches during the dissection. She wasn't much of an artist. But I was.

I dialed the phone.

"Fred," I said into the receiver. "Let's work on the field guide."

"Okay," he said.

"I wanna sketch the shark," I said.

"At the wharf?" he asked.

"Yeah."

"I'll meet you outside," he said.

I walked across the creaky floors to look out the window. In the light of the streetlamp, the leaves were bending upside down like it was going to rain. Mr. Patterson was on his porch, listening to the radios.

In the kitchen, I scanned the counter for my house key. I stuffed a sketch pad into my backpack and walked across the street.

"Any news about the shark?" I asked.

"Police are keeping watch," Mr. Patterson said.

"What are they waiting for?" I asked.

"Who knows? It's positively gothic."

"Any news about Dad?"

Mr. Patterson shook his head and pointed to the police scanner. "Still at the harbor."

Fred came out his front door.

"Fred!" I yelled. "Over here."

Fred changed course and walked next door to Mr. Patterson's.

"The shark's still there," I said to Fred, zipping my pack.

He raised his eyebrows.

"Let's go," I said.

He nodded.

Through the darkness, we rode our bikes into the wind down Beach Street, passing Front Beach and the old cemetery. The waves beat down on the sand louder at night, breaking even stronger than usual. At the Captain's Bounty Motor Inn, there were no guests on the balconies. We rounded the bend onto Main Street, past the bookstore, and coasted down the hill. The temperature had dropped. I regretted not packing a sweatshirt.

"It's definitely gonna rain," Fred said.

"I'll be quick," I said.

Our tires kicked up gravel that nicked my legs as we approached T Wharf. And right away, I saw the shark, still hanging over the water, like a torture victim. There was a Rockport Police squad car a stone's throw from the shark. I rode up to the window and peeked inside.

"Officer Parrelli!" I yelled. He was reading the newspaper by flashlight.

"Lucy, what are you doing here? It's late," he said. "Hi, Fred."

"You mind if we have a look at the shark?" I said.

"Go ahead. Then I'll give you guys a ride home. Storm's coming in."

I dropped the bike in the gravel and walked over to the shark. There was a tremendous fishy odor like a thousand tuna cans had been opened, and a sizable pool had formed on the ground below its mouth—blood, seawater, and mysterious shark fluids. Floodlights on the dock lit the corpse. I looked up at the shark's face, if that's what it was called.

A few of its teeth jutted out in crooked directions. The shark's mouthy expression and big black eyes looked human, as if it might strike up a conversation. *Mind if I eat your dad?*

The shark was anything but human. It was gigantic. There was a long tail and fins. It breathed underwater. I wasn't even sure it had bones.

The longer I stared at the eye, the more I thought it was really blue. Scars marked the snout, but one scar stood out from the rest—the letter *M*, with loopy humps like cursive.

Fred pointed to a small chunk missing from the dorsal fin.

"What happened there?" he asked.

"Don't know," I said, pulling my backpack over my shoulder. "Fight?"

I unzipped the bag and pulled out a pencil and the sketch pad.

"Freaky, isn't it?" Officer Parrelli said through the cruiser window.

"Yup," I said. "Sookie decide what he's going to do with it yet?"

"Tomorrow he'll cut it down and dispose of it. I think he's out celebrating tonight."

"Are you guarding it until then?" Fred asked.

"Yup. The captain's worried about weirdos trying to do something to it. But Sookie promised me a cooler full of lobsters if I sit here all night. You ready to go?"

"No," I said. "I just need a few minutes."

Fred crouched in front of me and I leaned into the sketch pad on his back.

I drew the strange arc of the shark's body in a single line like a big nose on the page, just for shape. I added the bands around the body and drew in the ropes that connected the shark to the winch, drawing the basic structure of the contorted shark to show how it was possible for something so large to be suspended in midair.

"What is she doing?" Officer Parrelli asked.

"Drawing the shark," Fred yelled over his shoulder.

"Why?"

"She's an artist," said Fred.

I smiled, filling in the fleshy bulges at the sides of the bands, and adding fins and teeth. I couldn't be too precious with the details once Fred's knees started shaking.

"Just one more minute," I said to him.

"Okay," he said.

The drawing looked a little cartoonish, but I felt like I had built the architecture of the scene. I could try to fill in the details later. We usually included one drawing of each animal in the field guide. I wondered whether I would record the contorted fish-out-of-water version of the shark, or if I should eventually draw something that showed the shark in a more natural position for the guide. All of the animals I had drawn before were alive.

I scratched Fred's head, to signal that I was finished.

"Thanks," I said.

"No problem," he said, turning around to get a look at the drawing. "Looks just like it."

I moved closer to the shark to get a better look at the ridges on the serrated teeth, leaning the sketch pad on my left forearm, to make a quick sketch of the steak-knife points. To the left of the shark drawing, the first raindrop hit the page. I finished up the teeth and a quick sketch of the eye before the drops started coming quickly.

"Get in the car, guys," said Officer Parrelli, popping the trunk of the cruiser.

I zipped up my backpack, just as the rain started pelting us.

"You could fit like four bodies in there," I said, as Officer Parrelli hefted my bike into the trunk.

He gave me a look.

"It was a joke," I said.

As we pulled away, I looked out the window at the

shark. The rain had picked up and was pelting the snout. The nasty puddle beneath it was growing.

There were three things on my mind, tangled up like necklaces in a jewelry box—my mom looking me in the eye, the shark that was hanging in the rain, and the empty house I was returning to. None of these felt like problems I could solve.

I hugged the backpack to my chest and looked at the rain sheeting on the window.

"She said she wasn't afraid to swim with them," I said.

"What?" Fred asked, turning to me from looking out his side of the cruiser.

"My mom," I said. "She wasn't afraid to swim with sharks."

"Yeah, I always thought that was kinda crazy," he said.

"Me too," I said, relieved that Fred felt the same way. "But they left her alone. Maybe she knew how to blend in."

"Probably," he said. "It shook you up when you saw her on TV."

"What do you mean?" I asked, knowing exactly what he meant.

"You dropped the phone," he said. "Are you okay?"

I could see Officer Parrelli's eyes looking at me in the rearview mirror.

"It took me off guard," I said. "I'd been thinking about her today because of the shark. When I saw her on TV, it was like she'd read my mind."

Fred breathed out through his mouth and looked me in the eye. He didn't know what to say, but he put his hand against the side of my leg and we just rode like that until the cruiser stopped on the narrow street between our houses.

"Stay in tonight," said Officer Parrelli, as he popped the trunk, rain bouncing off the carpet inside. "Go watch TV."

"Sure," I said. "Thanks for the ride."

The wind caught the heavy car door and it slammed shut behind me. Fred and I got soaked, pulling the bikes out of the trunk. I was worried about my sketch pad getting wet through the canvas backpack. Fred closed the trunk and Officer Parrelli rolled down the end of Smith Street, making a right toward town again.

"I'll see you tomorrow," I yelled to Fred over the loud rain, as we stood on my side of the road. A narrow river of water ran down the driveway onto Smith Street.

"You wanna watch the rest of the game at my house?" he said.

I shook my head. "It'll be a rainout, or something. I'll be fine."

"Call you in the morning," he said. "Don't let your drawings get wet."

"I know." I ran down the driveway.

Dad's car wasn't in the garage. I leaned my bike against the lawnmower and let myself into the house.

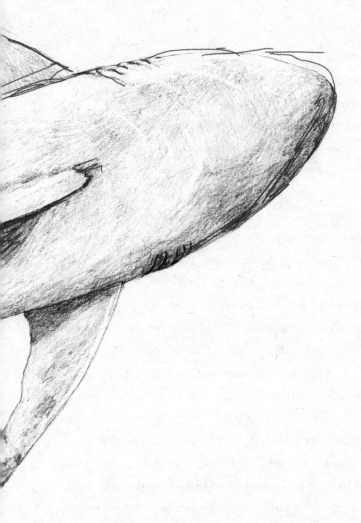

6. Emergency Contacts

I GRABBED A TOWEL FROM THE BATHROOM, WRAPPED IT around myself like a cape, and flopped into a chair at the kitchen table, thinking about what Officer Parrelli had said. *Tomorrow Sookie will cut down it down and dispose of it.*

I went into the kitchen and looked at the phone numbers on the wall, next to a framed picture of Mom and me. There was a list on white paper, stuck to the wall with yellowed Scotch tape that my grandmother—my mother's mother—had written years ago. Police, fire, Helen and Tom, Ernie and Bea—all the people she might need to call if she needed help. When my grandmother got sick, my parents came and they stayed. And I was born in this house, the year after she died.

There was another list of phone numbers in my mother's handwriting. I bet my mom couldn't take down her mother's list when she put up her own. Sookie was fourth on Mom's list, though I had never dialed his number before.

It was hard to tell which one of my parents had been closer to Sookie. He and my dad grew up on the same street and were best friends. My dad introduced Sookie to my mom in high school and the three of them became close. I remember coming into the kitchen one time and seeing

Sookie and Mom sharing a whole pie, laughing about something I didn't know anything about.

I picked up the phone and punched in Sookie's number, wrapping the cape over my shoulders again.

In the space between the last digit and the first ring, I practiced my line.

"I think you should call a biologist," I whispered.

But it rang and rang. There was no answer.

7. *Isopods*

IN THE MORNING, I THREW SMALL ROCKS AT FRED'S WINDOW from the wet road below. The storm had blown out the July humidity, leaving behind clean air and a dirty road. My foot slipped on mud as I chucked another pebble at Fred's house.

Fred's window slid open and his face moved in toward the screen. I could hear Zeppelin coming from his room.

"Morning," he said.

"Why do you listen to that stuff? It's OLD," I said, staring up at him while shielding my eyes with my palm.

"Because it's GOOD," he said.

I shrugged. "Big storm."

"I know," he said. "Did your dad make it home?"

"Yup. About two thirty this morning."

"And he's back at work already?"

"Yup. You free?"

"Sure. What do you want to do?" he asked.

"I want to talk to Sookie. Let's go down to the dock."

"Okay. Let me just get ready."

"Fred," I called out. "Can you bring me something for breakfast?"

"Sure," he said, before walking away from the open

window. I was so hungry, he could have brought me a plate of grass and I'd eat it.

There were branches in the street. I pushed a couple of them to the side of the narrow road as I walked over to Mr. Patterson's porch to wait for Fred.

"Morning, Mr. P," I said, climbing up the stairs. Mr. Patterson was sitting on the porch, in a pair of pants with no wrinkles and a collared shirt. It wasn't that he was into ironing his *slacks*, as he would call them. They were just made of synthetic material that never wrinkled. It was big in the 1970s, "which must have been when he stopped shopping," my mother had once said. "Probably not long before Mrs. Patterson died."

He might not have cared about his clothes anymore, but his hair was always combed into a neat white hairdo. Fred and I liked Mr. Patterson. He was never too busy to talk.

"Hello, Lucy. Did you lose power last night?"

I took a seat. The police radio farted. "We must have. The clock was blinking this morning. I slept through the whole thing."

"Well, then you missed a lot."

"Like what?" I asked, pointing to the scanner on the table between us.

"Trees down. Power outages. There was a break-in on Marmion Way," he said, pointing southeast. "And the shark is gone."

My stomach bottomed out. "Sookie took it down?" I asked.

"No. That's the unusual thing. They have been saying on the radio that Sookie reported it missing."

"Where did it go?" I asked.

"The police don't know yet," he said, shaking his head.

Fred's screen door slammed shut and Fred walked out into the street before spotting me on Mr. Patterson's porch. He came jogging up the steps and handed me a bagel wrapped in tinfoil. It was still warm from the toaster.

"Thanks," I said, unwrapping the package.

"What are you guys talking about?" He looked from Mr. Patterson's face to mine, which must have looked confused. Fred's brow furrowed.

"The shark is gone," I said, my lips slick with salty butter.

"What?"

"And Sookie doesn't know anything about it."

In seconds, Fred and I were on our bikes. I steered with one hand and ate the bagel with the other. The storm had made a mess of the beach, dredging up everything in the ocean and dumping it on the sand—seaweed, logs, and trash. The sewer drain sounded like a river.

Even though it was barely nine, tourists were just beginning to clog the sidewalks. We rode on the narrow street, past the big white Congregational church and the Art Association. The door to Tuck's Candies was wide-open. I could smell chocolate as we whizzed by. Fred and I coasted downhill, whirring like ghosts as we curved right at the fork. We turned onto the wharf. Two Rockport PD cruisers sat by the hoist. Sookie stood with his father, Paulie, and Lester. The straps that had suspended the shark from the hoist had been sliced and frayed. They dangled in a sinister way. The shark was really gone.

We crossed the gravel lot to the dock where the fishermen stood.

"Where's the shark?" I asked, looking from Sookie to Officer Parrelli. They looked like opposites—Sookie with bedhead and Officer Parrelli in uniform.

"It's gone," Sookie said.

"What do you mean, *gone*?"

"I mean *gone*," he repeated, irritated. Sookie touched the torn strap.

I looked at Officer Parrelli. "What happened? I thought you were watching the shark?"

"There was a break-in on Marmion Way. People take precedence over dead sharks, Lucy."

Fred was looking up at the straps, shielding his eyes from the sun. "Do you think someone took it?" he asked.

"We don't know yet," Officer Parrelli answered. "Something must have happened during the night. It could have been a prank, but it'd be next to impossible to move that shark."

Officer Parrelli walked over to his cruiser and sat in the front seat with the door open, scrawling something in a notebook. I scooted my bike up to Sookie and Paulie. Sookie's face looked redder than usual.

Sookie turned to Paulie. "I don't know what's worse—some moron stealing my shark or hauling that thing twenty miles to shore only to have it fall in the harbor."

I could tell that Sookie was in a mood, and while I wanted to bombard him with questions, I figured it was the wrong time. Besides, Officer Parrelli was striding across the gravel lot toward us. Sookie headed him off.

"Anything else? I gotta go make some money. It's already too friggin' late in the day."

"No, nothing new. Maybe I will have something for you by the time you come back to the wharf."

Sookie nodded, and he and Paulie set off for the boat.

"Bye," I said.

Paulie turned around and waved.

"See you, Lucy," Sookie said.

Officer Parrelli drove away.

"What do you think happened?" I asked Fred.

He looked up at the hoist with the frayed straps hanging down. "I don't know, Lucy. Remember how many guys it took to carry that thing? I don't know how anyone would have left the parking lot with the shark without being seen. This town has like a million eyes in the summer and all of the houses are on top of each other. I bet something happened during the storm."

"Well, what if it fell in the water? Then what?"

"Then it becomes food for the scavengers—the isopods."

"What's an isopod?"

"They look like giant wood lice. They eat carcasses of big fish and whales."

I held up my hands to stop him from explaining. "What a waste."

I dumped my bike and walked over to the edge of the lot and peered into the water. I half expected to see the shark's white belly stretched out at the bottom of the harbor, as though its weight had split the bands and the shark had just sunk to the seafloor. But it was too green and murky to see anything.

"If I ever need to dispose of evidence, that's where I'm going to put it," I said, as I headed back to Fred and righted my bike.

"I guess we don't need a biologist anymore," I said.

Fred looked as though he might cry.

8. Real Women

I THINK LOSING THE SHARK BOTHERED FRED SO MUCH THAT he had to get out of Rockport, even for a day. He'd been sitting on his birthday money for a month, waiting for Fiona to take us on the train into the city, to Newbury Comics, to browse through music, comic books, and assorted thingamajigs. When she finally had nothing better to do, she sat beside us on the commuter rail into North Station. We followed her underground like baby mice to the Green Line and the Red Line, until we popped out on a dirty street in crowded Harvard Square.

Fred took the lead and we headed for The Garage, the sound of drumsticks on buckets fading away. I was annoyed because I'd wanted to stop at the art store for some pens for the field guide with the money my dad had given me—a ten-minute mission. But going to a music store with Fred required extreme patience. It was as if he looked at every album in the store before making a decision. He could spend hours there. Fiona looked back at me and rolled her eyes, trying to keep pace.

The Garage was an old parking ramp that had been converted to a mini-mall. It wound in a spiral, with stores and restaurants on different levels. The smell of pizza instantly made me want to eat. Fred was practically running, as we hiked uphill to get to the top. When we finally leveled off, my legs were burning.

"What's he looking for?" Fiona asked.

"I don't know," I said.

Fred passed under the neon letters over the store entrance like he was crossing a finish line. The music from Newbury Comics spilled into The Garage, becoming louder as Fiona and I followed Fred inside. The store was large, but it didn't take me long to spot the back of his head in the jazz section. Fred had played trumpet in the school jazz band since sixth grade, but he didn't listen to jazz at home. Fred liked Led Zeppelin and Pink Floyd and a bunch of other old bands that I could barely tolerate. I decided to give him a few minutes to find what he was looking for before dragging him out to get some pizza.

While we waited, Fiona spun a rack of sunglasses, and the next thing I knew, we were trying on pairs together. Fiona was the art-school version of Snow White with short black hair, ivory skin, and glossy rosebud lips. She could turn a pillowcase into a skirt and make it look like it belonged in a magazine. Fiona put on a pair of sci-fi sunglasses that were just a bar across her eyes. I would've never noticed them if Fiona hadn't put them on first. On her face, they were the perfect balance of weird and cool. I grabbed the exact glasses and put them on.

"Twins," I said, looking into the mirror. Except they

looked completely different on me. It was like she was the front woman of a punk band and I was a pubescent alien. We laughed.

"These," she said, as she slid a new pair of frames onto my face, giving me goose bumps.

I looked in the mirror again. She nodded.

I looked at the lavender, cat's eye glasses. As a rule, I didn't like pink and purple, but the color made my red hair pop. I looked at Fiona like she was some kind of a witch.

Wearing the glasses, I wandered into the comic-book section of the store and randomly pulled a comic off a rack. *The Punisher War Journal.* There was a heavily armed woman on the cover, screaming. It looked like she was literally jumping into a disaster, wearing a black scuba suit and a red jacket that a piano teacher would wear for a holiday recital. On her torso, there was a white skull that matched the Marvel Punisher icon on the cover. Her breasts were the eyes of the skeleton face, which drew my eyes to them even faster.

"Real women don't look like that," Fiona said.

"I know."

Fiona was wearing a new pair of sunglasses with square lenses. She leaned over my shoulder. "*I* don't look like that," she said.

"Me either," I said. "What *am* I gonna look like?"

Fiona shrugged. "Probably like your mom."

"Do you look like your mom?" I asked.

"Sort of," she said. "Bodies change."

I looked at the comic-book woman's huge gun.

"She looks pretty tough, though," I said.

"Uh-huh."

I noticed the way the artist defined her huge muscles using light and dark and how her knee was foreshortened, just like we were taught in art class.

"She's flying off the page," I said. I wondered how I could do that with the shark in the field guide, show movement with just lines.

I flipped through the pages to see other examples.

"Real men don't look like that either," Fiona said.

She headed for the music section and I spotted Fred. He was still looking through a stack of albums.

"What'd you find?" I asked.

He did a double take and gave me a look. "Nice glasses."

I pulled the album from under his arm. Miles Davis. I glanced at the title: *Bitches Brew*. Fred knew that I hated the b-word. I looked at him and he shrugged apologetically.

I slid the glasses onto the top of my head. Fred often chose albums with interesting artwork, but this one was different. My eyes moved immediately from a flaming pink flower in the bottom left to a strange storm brewing in the top right. There were three African people on the cover: a woman with a serene face and two other people hugging in the bottom center. Then I realized they were looking out at a storm with fierce lightning in the distance. The artwork was colorful and surreal, and it left me feeling uneasy.

"Check out the back," Fred said.

I flipped over the cover and saw a pair of hands, one black and the other white. The hands were linked, but some of the fingers looked dislocated and each ring finger stretched like taffy, connecting into the line of a woman's chin.

"What does this mean?" I asked, looking up. "What is this?"

"It's jazz fusion."

"What's that?" I asked.

"It's jazz meets rock and roll."

"Is that gonna work?" I asked.

"Some people think it does."

I could tell by the way we'd traveled over three different MBTA lines to buy this album that Fred was one of those people.

"Where'd you hear about it?"

"A guy from the high school jazz band," he said. "I'll play it for you when we get home."

I shrugged. "I'm crabby. I need food."

"Okay, I'm almost ready to check out."

At the register, I looked at the rack of postcards. There were mostly black-and-white portraits of bands and a few famous paintings. Fred and Fiona looked at them too, while we waited in line.

"Miles," Fred shouted. He pulled out a close-up of Miles Davis, wearing some crazy glasses. They were like bug eyes, except they were a little square. They seemed too big for the man's face.

"I saw those," Fiona said. She headed for the rack of sunglasses and came back with a pair that almost matched the ones in the postcard photo. The frames were black and the lenses were tinted yellow. She unfolded the plastic arms and pushed them onto Fred's face.

We both looked at him, giggling. It was like he was wearing a diving mask. Fred laughed, but when it was his turn in line, he put the glasses on top of the postcard and the album. The guy behind the counter rang him up. Fiona returned our sunglasses to the rack.

Fred dropped the album and postcard into his backpack and put his glasses on his face.

"Pizza, then art store?" he asked, looking at me sincerely. I didn't know what to think of the glasses. They didn't seem like Fred.

I nodded.

o o ° o

That night, I sat on the rug in my room with my pencils and new black pens scattered on the floor. I flipped my sketch pad back to the drawings I'd made the night we saw the shark hanging from the winch. The shark was a bunched-up blob in the straps. I tried to imagine what it would look like stretched out, moving through the ocean, but when I drew more sharks on the page, I couldn't get them right. I erased the lines again and again.

I blew the dust into the air and heard strange sounds coming from outside. At first, I thought it was some kind of an animal. We had a lot of raccoons in town. I put my sketch pad on the rug and crawled to the window. At first, I searched for pairs of glowing eyes on the street, but like a magnet, I looked straight into Fred's room. The light was on and his window was open.

I heard a breathy trumpet sound that went flat and faded away. I made a mental note to tell him later that I'd thought he was a wounded rodent. There was a trumpet shriek, followed by a few notes strung together nicely. And then it went back to sounding like fourth-grade band practice.

I heard a number of sounds layered behind him—drums, a keyboard playing cosmic notes, and something low, like a saxophone. It sounded like they were all playing from different sheet music. Fred was that kid who always got picked to play the solos in the school band concerts. He could play any song that the band teacher gave him and it sounded good. But this was odd.

He was sitting on the edge of the bed, leaning over the trumpet.

In a way, he was playing along with the album, echoing the trumpet sounds he'd heard. Except, he'd play the same notes over and over, like he was trying to learn a different language. Everything sounded like mistakes.

I was ready to give up for the night. I clicked my pencil case shut and the music stopped. While I was putting the supplies back on my desk, a farty bass line came from Fred's room. He'd put on a new song and I liked it a little better, though I'd never heard it before either.

I peeked out the window again. Fred's trumpet lay on the bed. I leaned back a bit until I could see him. He was wearing his sunglasses, playing air bass, totally on another planet. I covered my mouth with my hand, so I wouldn't laugh or yell anything out the window.

The layers of instruments started to pile up. First bass, then drums, then guitar (maybe), and keyboards (maybe). It was hard to even name some of the instruments because the sounds they made were so unusual. Fred was still plucking imaginary strings to the looping rhythm. His hair flopped around and he danced like a robot that had been left out in the rain. Fred unrestrained was a good sight. He looked sort of disheveled and less uptight. And those sunglasses were growing on me. I had the urge to run over and kiss him, but I quickly stuffed it back in like a tampon flying out of my backpack.

He slowed down and fumbled in his pocket. *Puff.* Fred's face was red and he had a sweaty hairline. As he held his breath, he squinted in my direction, like maybe he had seen me. I hit the ground so fast, I got rug burn on my chin.

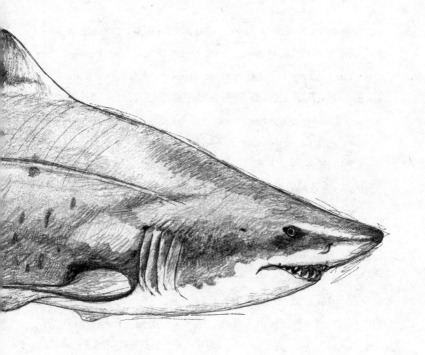

9. Moon Snail

AT LOW TIDE THE NEXT DAY, FRED ASKED IF WE COULD GO to Folly Cove. We'd been there more times than I could count. It was his favorite spot to collect specimens for the creepy aquarium that he kept in the garage. The aquarium looked more like a swamp than one of those pristine tanks at the dentist's office, but it made a nice temporary home for some of the field guide critters until I could get around to drawing them.

Fred grabbed a bucket and sandwiches from his house. I packed the sketch pad and met Fred out front with my bike. He was wearing his Miles Davis glasses.

"Hold on, you've got something in your hair," he said, scooting his bike a little closer. He zeroed in on my scalp and pinched a group of hairs at the root, sliding mysterious debris to the end and setting off a ripple of chills from my shoulders to my face. I looked into his palm.

"Just a leaf," he said. There was still junk falling out of the trees from the storm. I didn't care if it was a caterpillar or a bramble or lice. I just wanted him to do it again. But he pushed off with his foot and steadied his bike.

We pedaled down Smith Street and the ocean came into view. The water was gray-blue under the clearing sky. I led the way as we coasted by the parking meters along the edge of the beach. We had to swerve around branches from the storm.

We passed the gazebo at the end of our street where the American Legion band played every Saturday night of the summer and we crossed Beach Street. I watched the divers standing in the parking lot across from Back Beach. In the summer, there were always divers hanging around half dressed by the side of the road. It was a good spot for beginners because the cove was protected and it wasn't very deep.

Seven divers stood between the road and the shore. One man was zipping up a woman. They looked like carpenter ants in their black suits. I wondered if they were afraid to dive so close to the spot where a great white had been towed into the harbor.

We rode down Route 127 to Folly Cove, passing a mile of granite curbing and houses built with granite blocks. We coasted by the entrance to Halibut Point State Park where, some nights, Fred's sisters swam in the quarries. *Skinnydipped,* as Fred had once told me. I looked behind me even though I knew Fred was still there. I could hear his bucket thumping.

We ditched our bikes and started the trek to the big rocks at the edge of the tide, egg-shaped hunks of granite banging together underfoot. Offshore, an unfinished break wall was home to kelp beds and invertebrates. Divers loved that place too.

At mid-tide it was a difficult walk. The small rocks became big rocks. The brown boulders covered in slippery seaweed looked like hairy trolls, and the medium stones shifted below us.

"Did you hear me practicing my trumpet last night?" he asked.

I held my breath. He'd seen me in the window. "I heard *something*," I said, stepping carefully onto the rocks. "But it didn't sound like music."

"Thanks," he said. I could hear that he was a little hurt.

"No, it just sounds different," I said. I skimmed his arm with my palm, like an apology. "Were you trying to play along?"

"Sort of," he said.

"Do you listen to songs with words anymore?" I asked.

"Sometimes."

We wobbled to a point where the large rocks held a tide pool. I sat on a hunk of granite and put the sketch pad on my lap, opening to a drawing of the great white shark, with its pointy teeth and charcoal-black throat. I wondered what had happened to the shark, but I was pretty sure it was gone for good. If my mom had been there, I knew the shark wouldn't have gone to waste. I turned to a clean page.

"What are we looking for today?" I asked.

"Nothing in particular," he said, flipping his glasses onto his head. "Wait, check it out." Fred picked up a sea star, an amputee.

"How can they grow a new leg?" I said. "Why can't humans do that?"

"They've just figured it out," Fred said. "Your dad told me a story once about oyster fishermen. The fishermen were pissed at the sea stars for eating their oysters, so they cut off the sea stars' arms and threw them back into the ocean. Only, it doubled the number of sea stars and destroyed the oysters."

"Bad karma," I said, doodling a group of sea stars in the corner of my paper, attacking a single oyster. "Mind if I break into the sandwiches?"

"Go ahead," he said, searching the pool.

I grabbed a paper bag from the bucket and looked inside. There were two turkeys on wheat, a couple of apples at the bottom, and two granola bars. I took a sandwich out of the wax paper bag and got down to business. Both Fred and I liked our sandwiches dry—no mustard, no mayo.

Fred found a moon snail with a shell the size of a baseball. We had a moon snail page in the field guide already, but this specimen was freakishly large. The bucket contained about a gallon of seawater, and Fred set the moon snail at the bottom while he grabbed his tools. While chomping on an apple, I looked down at the snail and drew a large circle around and around until I made the circuit five times with my pen. In the middle of my circle, I made a tight spiral pattern that spread into a wide band to join the circle's edge. The core of the moon snail's spiral was blue while most of the shell was orange. Who picked these colors? It was a strange choice because they were opposites—but it worked.

Fred sat down beside me on the rock, holding a measuring tape from his mom's sewing kit. He pulled the moon snail out of the bucket. I drew Fred's hand holding the specimen, his thumb curving around the side and his fingertips peeking around the other side of the shell. I'd been working on hands all year long. I was getting pretty good. I carried his wrist down the page for a little bit. It looked small under his chunky watch.

I wished I'd brought colored pencils. He leaned over my drawing while I made notes about the shell colors in the margin. I could feel his cheek near my shoulder.

"How do you do that?" he asked.

I looked at him. "Do what?"

"Draw things that look three-D."

I shrugged. "I'm an art person. You are a science person."

"You don't think you are a science person?"

"Not really."

"Why not?"

"I don't like equations," I said. I thought for a minute. "But if you could tell science like a story, I'd pay attention. I liked your story about the sea stars and the oysters."

"I can tell a story about the moon snail."

"Go ahead," I said.

He grabbed the moon snail out of the bucket.

"Okay. Look at the shell. It's an example of the golden ratio—an equiangular spiral, based on the proportion of one to one-point-six-one-eight—"

"First of all, you should skip eighth grade and go to MIT. Second of all, you sound like a robot. What does that mean?"

"It means the spiral on the shell is made in perfect proportion. Don't you ever see a living thing and wonder how it was made?"

"Sometimes." I thought about the shark's endless rows of teeth. "But that's still not a story," I said.

He thought for a minute. "Okay. I got one. You know when you are looking for shells on the beach and you find one with a perfect hole in it?"

I nodded. I knew exactly what he was talking about. "I used to string them on yarn and make necklaces."

"Right. Do you know how that hole got there?"

I shook my head.

"It was the moon snail."

I squinted at Fred.

"It has this tool like a drill that's kind of like a tongue, but not a tongue. And it has teeth all over it. The snail drills the hole and excretes an enzyme to soften the shell and then it eats the clam."

I hated to admit it, but I had wondered on several occasions how that hole got there. It was like a mystery solved. I smiled at Fred. "That's a story. You win."

He smiled back. "I have lots of them."

"No more numbers though."

"Just wait. You'll come around," he said.

That's the thing about Fred. I always believed every word he said. Not only was he smart about academic stuff. He was smart about me. If he predicted that I would like numbers someday, I would be open to the idea. That donkey.

"Aren't you eating anything?" I asked, moving on to the granola bar.

Fred dropped the snail in the pool. It made a noise like a tub of Vaseline falling into the toilet. I was staring at him for a long time, but he wouldn't look my way. He was too busy frisking a pile of seaweed. Finally, he stood up and caught my gaze.

I smiled at him. "I feel pretty blah about the shark."

"Blah?"

"Disappointed. 'Cause it's gone," I said.

"Really?" he said, which was fair because I had never taken much of an interest in biology before. "Me too. We can still work on the field guide. I'll come over tonight. We can look through your mom's old books for shark facts."

I thought about how those weighty biology texts that I had used to press flowers or smooth bent photographs had served other purposes for her. I was curious.

"Okay," I said.

He pulled his sunglasses down from his head and they settled on his face.

"What? They look cool," he said.

I looked skeptical.

The only thing *cool* was Fred's confidence that he looked cool.

10. *Meatballs*

LATER IN THE AFTERNOON, WE HEADED HOME. FRED VEERED off to his side of the street, his bucket of snails sloshing.

"We're working on the field guide later, right?" he asked.

"Yup," I said. "Come over after dinner."

Dad's old Volvo was parked in the driveway. I saw the grocery bags in the trunk and I ditched my bike under the pine tree. I grabbed one of the paper bags and looked inside, heading for the house. Dad opened the screen door on his way back to the car.

"Hi," he said. "How was your day?"

"Better now," I said.

When the bags were gathered on the kitchen floor, I started pulling groceries onto the kitchen table—half a watermelon, a coffee cake, milk, and ground beef.

"Lucy," he said, putting a pizza in the freezer. "I'm sorry I let the refrigerator get so bare."

"Is everything okay?" I asked.

He thought for a minute. "Sometimes I can't get it all done," he said. "It's been a busy summer for the dive team. But I'm making meatballs for dinner."

I gave him a hug and just stayed there like I was hanging on to a buoy.

"I was going to make something from there," he said, pointing to the Silver Palate cookbook on the table. "But that's too much work tonight."

I knew exactly what he meant. When I let go of Dad, I brought the watermelon over to the counter and unwrapped the plastic, dripping pink juice into the sink. I sliced the watermelon half into quarters and cut the fruit into thick wedges. I wrapped one in a paper towel and brought it upstairs, sucking away the juice. I couldn't stand hanging around downstairs while Dad cooked the onions for the meatballs. I was so hungry for real food that it made me dizzy.

o o º o

At dinner, Dad told me that he knew what happened to the shark. He ran into Officer Parrelli at the IGA.

"First thing in the morning, Parrelli got a call from a man in Pigeon Cove, complaining about a horrible fish odor coming from his neighbor's yard," Dad said. "But when the Rockport PD went to investigate, it was just trash from a lobster bake. The storm had stirred up the neighbor's garbage and dumped it all over the side yard next to the caller's house."

"Gross," I said.

"Then there was a call from a woman who'd seen her neighbor pull into his driveway sometime in the night with a trailer and something under a tarp, but it turned out to be a Jet-Ski."

I rolled my eyes and wondered how many ridiculous phone calls the Rockport Police Department must receive in an average week.

"But later, one of the officers took a call from a guy who lives on Bearskin Neck. He was up in the night 'cause a storm surge made the tide come right into the lower level of the house."

"I wouldn't want to live that close to the harbor," I said.

"No," Dad said.

"Anyway, the guy ran to the upper level to call his brother for help and he saw the shark swinging from the hoist. Said it was like a giant punching bag, knocking back and forth. And in one big gust, the straps snapped and the shark fell into the harbor."

My eyes bugged out. "Do you think it's still in the harbor?"

Dad shook his head. "That shark's probably in Guam right now."

I felt the meatballs sitting in my stomach. "So it's gone," I said.

"It's gone," he said.

"Does Sookie know?" I asked.

"Yeah, I'm pretty sure he does."

I imagined Sookie's blood vessels popping when he heard the news. The shark was headed to Guam, and the biologists would never get to look for whatever it was that they looked for inside of a dead shark. Fred would not be happy.

"Why are you so quiet?" he asked, scraping the plate with his fork.

"No reason," I said.

"Is it about the shark?"

"Sort of."

11. *Clasperhead!*

BY THE TIME FRED SHOWED UP THAT NIGHT, I HAD NEARLY eaten myself sick. I followed up a solid base of meatballs with a couple of packaged cupcakes and washed them down with a can of cream soda.

"Are you okay?" he asked when I answered the door.

I shrugged. "Stomachache."

He nodded. His sunglasses were on top of his head like a hair accessory. It was almost dark outside.

I told him about the shark falling from the winch and possibly being whisked away to Guam in the rough seas. He frowned. "I guess it makes more sense than someone stealing it."

"Yeah," I said. "You still want to put it in the field guide though, right?"

He held up his backpack. "Yup. I brought everything over."

"You'll have to show me where the shark books are," I said, walking up the stairs. I had a vague idea of where they were in the office, but I didn't know our library as well as Fred did. He borrowed our books all the time.

I flipped the switch on the wall and track lighting illuminated three columns of floor-to-ceiling bookshelves. These were mostly my mom's books, but Dad opened them every once in a while to learn about the things he dredged up while scuba diving.

Fred sprawled himself on the floor and began working on a new page in our field guide. He wrote "White Shark" at the top and "Date Sighted: July 9." He recorded basic shark stats from one of my mom's books and left a big space for me to draw an image of the great white. I needed to find a book that had a better picture of a great white to sketch than the headshot in Fred's book.

"Any recommendations?" I asked.

"Try the bottom shelf."

One of the books was written by Cousteau and Cousteau, which looked interesting because I had at least heard of one of the Cousteaus. I cracked open my art box and dug for the turquoise pencils. We stretched out on the floor. Fred paged through the shark encyclopedia. I put my sketch pad so close to Fred that when I belly-flopped onto the rug, I could have knocked him out. With our feet touching, we set to work. Fred jotted down notes from one of the books on to his paper. I looked at photographs in Cousteau and Cousteau's book, stopping at page thirty to look at a strange photograph.

A sand shark was spread on the ground, cut cleanly down the middle. A woman with pigtails pried opened one of the flaps of skin and muscle, revealing the insides of the abdomen—orange organs; pink, fleshy walls; and stripes of blood. Her mouth was wide-open as she looked at more than a dozen baby sharks, pouring out of the hole in their mother.

Among other things, the caption read, *The mother shark, after giving birth, will not eat for days in the area where she gave birth, so as not to eat her babies by mistake.*

I had two thoughts. *Do the father sharks ever eat the baby sharks? And was Sookie's shark a female?*

"Listen to this," Fred said, reading from his book. "'White sharks are warm-blooded, but their hearts and gills keep the temperature of the water.'"

"What? Why?" I asked.

"'The elevated visceral temperature also helps the shark digest food and increase the developmental processes of the babies in a warm uterus.'"

I put my head on his shoulder for a moment.

"I love that you can just throw around 'uterus.' You are highly evolved."

I looked at the page Fred was reading. My eyes zeroed in on a sentence. My mom had always used anatomical names for private parts, but for some reason, seeing *vagina* in print while lying on the floor with Fred seemed indecent. "Oh my God. Some sharks have two vaginas," I said.

I turned and looked at him, my eyes open wide. Fred was smiling. His face was so close, I could smell his sunscreen.

"And two penises. They're called claspers," Fred added, raising his eyebrows.

"Clasper? What?! Why?" I asked.

"Maybe to make sure everything works out," he said. "They probably don't have a lot of chances to get it right."

"Why didn't you tell me this before?!" I said, bumping his leg with my foot.

"You never asked," he said, turning his face back to the book.

This was too weird for me. My cheeks were starting to feel warm. "Clasperhead!" I yelled at Fred.

He caught on quick. "Clasperweed!"

I disgusted him at *clasperless*, and research resumed. Though I kept calling out new ones as they came to me.

He started unconsciously tapping his toe on my toe while he scrawled more notes onto the paper. Then this buzz radiated up my calves like a spark climbing a long fuse up my gangly legs, tripping off a series of flashes in my thighs and shoulders. Lately I was hypersensitive to touch and even someone else combing my hair or scratching my back felt like a transformer blowing up under my skin. Fred kept tapping. I didn't move my foot. I let the waves ripple up the back of my neck. But he just read and scrawled notes on his pad.

I rolled onto my back, put my knees up like I was ready to do sit-ups and sighed. "Clasperface." Staring up at the ceiling, I asked, "Why sharks? Why'd she pick sharks?"

"Who?"

"My mom."

"Because they are sharks," he said. Duh.

"So?"

"They have been here since the dinosaurs, but we know

almost nothing about them—white sharks especially." He rolled over. "Think how cool it would be if you were one of the people to make a big discovery. And maybe one of those discoveries could help protect the species."

"Do you think my mom made any discoveries?"

"Yup. You should talk to your dad," he said, taking his inhaler out of his pocket.

Fred pulled himself off the rug and took a puff. He walked in an arc around the books and papers spread on the floor, before standing in front of the bookshelves. Maybe it was because his brain was cloudy from the lack of oxygen, but he stared a little too long at a row of cardboard file holders, labeled by year, containing folders and spiral-bound stacks of paper.

He removed 1991, the most recent set. "Ever look in here?" he asked me, holding the file box for me to see.

I shook my head. He put the box on the floor and flipped through the stack.

"Your mom's name is on every single one of them. They look like reports," he said. "'Reproductive Behavior and Social Organization of Dogfish.' It's from January 1991."

"Seriously?" I shrug. "Dogfish should *stop* reproducing."

"What?" He looked at me like I was nuts. "What are the larger sharks going to eat if there are no dogfish?" he persisted.

"People," I said.

He rolled his eyes and resumed looking through the stack, which made me feel worse. I wanted him to put the reports down. What was so interesting about dogfish? And who cared about their social lives?

Fred was unmoved by my defensive behavior. He yanked out the last report in the set. "This one says, 'Proposal for Cape Cod White Shark and Gray Seal Study.'"

He opened the front cover, scanned the table of contents, and flipped through the pages.

"What's the date?" I asked.

"May 1991."

My mom died in June 1991.

She would have just finished pulling together the proposal, poking the holes on the left-hand side of the pages, and binding the paper with a black plastic spiral. I wondered if she had ever submitted the proposal. It was probably too soon to have heard back from anyone by the day she died.

"Do you mind if I borrow this?" Fred asked, holding up the last research proposal she wrote.

My brain was underwater. "What?" I asked.

The 1991 box was like the kite on a snapped string, a loose piece of her that Fred had caught. It was her words, recorded at the point when she was as old as she was ever going to get. I felt like an outsider. He found a treasure. But why did he want her words? What did she say?

I looked at Fred, hanging on to May 1991. I wanted to rip it out of his hands, but I said, "You have to give it back."

He must have heard desperation in my voice. Because he looked me in the eye and said, "Don't worry. I will."

12. *Circle of Willis*

ONE SUMMER DAY, WHEN I WAS SEVEN, MY MOM DROVE TO the Cape in the early morning, boarded a research boat in Chatham, and left shore with four other scientists and a boat captain. As usual, they were looking for sharks.

Sometime after lunch, she developed a terrible headache and started vomiting. The scientists knew something was very wrong. They didn't know an aneurysm had ruptured in the network of blood vessels at the bottom of her brain called the circle of Willis. It didn't help her chance of survival that she was more than ten miles from the mainland when the captain signaled the Coast Guard and turned the boat around.

I was at day camp, listening to the counselor read *Julie of the Wolves*.

Dad was interviewing a robbery witness in Salem.

It was a clear and breezy day.

And then one of the scientists called my dad. He drove to the Cape alone, while Mr. Patterson picked me up from camp. We sat on his porch, while I looked at my house across the street. The old man was straight with me.

"Something happened in her brain when she was on the boat, Lucy."

"Is she going to be okay?" I asked.

He shook his head. "The doctors think she was already gone before the medics arrived."

I looked at him, confused. Gone where?

"She died," he said. He rubbed my back with one hand and covered his eyes with the other. I felt like the air was stuck in my chest, half used.

Sometimes I wonder why Mr. Patterson broke the news instead of my dad, but when my mom collapsed on the boat, things stopped happening in the usual way. She didn't finish her research. She didn't come home for a late dinner. She didn't come home at all.

13. *The Quarry*

THAT SATURDAY NIGHT, FRED CALLED ME OVER TO HIS house to continue working on the field guide. I packed my bag. Mr. Patterson sat on his porch, cleaning his French horn with a white cloth.

"What's in the bag?" he asked.

"Books, art supplies, clothes."

"You running away?"

"No. Just going to Fred's."

"I knew my wife before we were in grammar school. She lived on the corner," he said, pointing up the street. "We used to go clamming. Then one day, she looked different to me. I asked if I could escort her to a party. The rest is history."

"Yeah, I gotta go." It was too weird of a conversation to be having with Mr. Patterson.

"Life is a long time."

"Suppose so," I said. Then I gestured to the horn. "You playing tomorrow night?"

"Sunday, isn't it?"

I nodded. Mr. Patterson played in a band every Sunday night of the summer, in the gazebo at the end of our street with the rest of the old American Legion guys. Fred and I stopped to listen every once in a while. And Fred always watched the brass players with a critical eye.

"See ya around," I said, heading up Fred's walk.

I knocked on the front door, but there was no answer, so I let myself in and pounded upstairs. If I knew what I was doing, I could have put together four complete outfits from all of the clothing and jewelry strewn on the hallway floor. I followed the music on the radio to the open bathroom door. Bridget sat on the toilet lid, lacquering her nails with ballet pink, the radio perched behind her on top of the tank. Fiona curled her eyelashes in the mirror. They were Irish twins, seventeen and sixteen.

"Hi, Lu," said Bridget, dipping her brush into the polish, blowing like an oscillating fan over her nails.

Based on the amount of junk cluttering the counter—hairspray, plastic clips, cotton balls—it was either fixing to be a big night, or they were wasting a lot of time on preparation to just hang out and watch TV. Fiona pumped a couple of shots of hair gel into her hand and worked the blob into her wet hair. She reached for a plastic tray of cosmetics, the compacts clicking and bumping against each other as she dug for the right color.

"Want me to do your makeup?" she asked, turning to face me. I wanted to tell her she could do anything to me that she pleased, as long as I came out looking remotely like her.

"Uh, sure," I said.

"Sit here," Bridget said as she rose from the toilet lid, flapping her hands before taking her spot in front of the mirror.

Fiona hummed along with the radio as she looked me over.

Fiona's face was close. It made me feel awkward, like I didn't know whether to track her eyes or stare off into space. I zeroed in on the linen cabinet behind her, which reminded me of the day when I got my first period. I had been home alone and of course there was nothing under our bathroom sink except a barf bowl and some Q-Tips. So I had wadded up half a roll of toilet paper, stuffed it between my legs, and went across the street to Fred's.

Fred had opened the door when I'd knocked. I'd asked him if any of the females in the house were available. Of course they weren't, so I marched up to the bathroom without saying a word. The linen cabinet had been stuffed with feminine hygiene supplies, a city of boxes. I'd grabbed a few of each variety and stuffed them into my shorts, saving one pad to wear home.

When I'd opened the door, Fred was standing there.

"I got my period," I'd told him.

"Oh," he'd said. And I was surprised by how unaffected he'd seemed, like I'd told him I'd replaced the toilet paper roll.

He'd put his hand on my shoulder, to gently move me aside and started digging in the linen cabinet.

"What are you doing?" I'd asked.

"Here," he'd said, handing me a bottle of Midol.

"What's this for?" I'd asked, though I'd seen it on TV.

"It 'relieves the symptoms of premenstrual syndrome'," he read from the bottle.

"But I think I have *menstrual* syndrome," I'd said.

He'd shook his head and pushed the bottle into my hand. "I think it's all the same."

o o º o

Fiona swabbed my eyelids with a tiny foam brush rolled in apricot powder and drew on top of my lash line with a brown pencil.

"Hold still."

Every time she moved toward the tear ducts my eyeballs went spastic. When Fiona came near me with the mascara wand, it was like having a mini-blackout, this dark clot closing in before my eyes shut.

"Shoot," she said, licking her finger and wiping the gook off the side of my nose.

She stepped back and looked at one eye, then the other, and back again before raising her brows.

"Looks okay."

Fiona fumbled through the compacts again.

"I have a lot of freckles," I said apologetically.

"I noticed," she said, rubbing a cake of honey-colored blush with a soft brush. "I'm not going to cover them up."

"Isn't that what makeup is for?" I asked.

Fiona looked at me. "Why would you want to cover up

your freckles?" she asked. "That's who you are. They're beautiful."

Fiona gently swept my cheeks with the powder. It felt like balls of dandelion seeds passing over my face and I shivered, which made Fiona stop.

"You okay?"

"Yeah, it feels nice." I instantly worried that might be a weird thing to say. Fiona pressed on.

Fred appeared in the doorway. "What are you *doing* to her?"

"It's just makeup, Fred," I said, my voice a little distorted from my chin being pressed up into the air.

"Yeah, but you look fine." I could tell by the wrinkled brow and whiny tone that he was bothered by the fact that Fiona was doing my makeup. Maybe he was worried that it would make me one of them. I didn't care that they were putting makeup on me. I just liked the attention.

Fiona dialed up a half inch of coral lipstick from a black tube and said, "Go like this," pushing her lips out into a pout. I did as she said and she dabbed it onto my mouth.

"Now go like this." She rubbed her lips together and opened and closed them like a goldfish.

"I thought we were going to work on the field guide," Fred said.

"I will. I'll be done in a minute," I said.

"She's having fun, Freddy. Relax," Bridget said, curling iron in hand, nearly frying her dirty-blond hair, elbow out like a salute. It smelled like hot hair, nail polish remover, and a soft perfume, which Bridget had sprayed on at least eight out of twenty pulse points.

"This song is terrible," Fred said, returning to his room. I felt like I should follow him, but Fiona was almost done with me. She handed me a mirror. I focused on my eyes at first, surprised by the thick line under my lashes, but the overall look was warm and clear, maybe even pretty. My freckles and red hair were still there and I looked at myself for a moment instead of turning away.

Fiona smiled. "You look great."

"Her eyes are a little too much," said Bridget, unfurling a boingy strip of hair.

I heard feet pounding up the stairs, in a one-two rhythm that signaled Maggie's arrival to the second floor. She stood in the doorway with both feet planted. She stared at me.

"You look nice, Lucy." I couldn't tell if she was sincere, but it sounded positive the way her voice went up at the end of my name. Then she looked at me quizzically. "Who did her? Her eyes are too dark."

She grabbed a tissue off the counter for me and demonstrated how to peel off the top layer of eye makeup without losing the whole look.

"All right, what are your plans?" she asked Bridget and Fiona.

Silence. Fiona placed each case back into the cosmetic tray, one by one.

"A bunch of us are going over to Lauren's house to watch a movie," Bridget offered.

"Does 'a bunch of us' include Dominick Maffeo?"

Dominick was Bridget's new boyfriend. Dominick's father owned a Sicilian bakery in Gloucester. Everyone thought he was a decent guy, but Maggie Kelly had sonar for boys who were interested in her girls and she was picking up a strong reading on Dominick.

Maggie looked back at me and said, "You're taking Lucy and Fred."

"What?" Fred yelled from his room before thundering down the hall, inhaler in hand. *Puff.*

Fiona looked into the mirror and made eye contact with Bridget.

"Mom, come on!" Bridget pleaded, leaning the hot rod on its kickstand. "That's ridiculous."

"No it's not. If you are just watching a movie, there's no reason why the kids can't tag along. I'm sure your friends will understand. End of story."

"We are busy!" Fred bellowed. "Lucy and I have things to do. *You* go babysit Fi and Bridget."

"There's an idea," Maggie said, standing up straight. "Take your pick. It's me or Fred."

o o o o

An hour later we were in Dominick's car headed to swim at the quarries. This had been the plan all along, though the guest list had to be revised. Even though the weather had cleared by the end of the day, there was still a cool damp-ness outside that made me want to go in the water even less than normal.

"Why did we spend all that time putting on makeup and doing hair if we were just going swimming?" I asked Fiona, who sat with Fred and me in the back.

She shrugged. "What else we got to do?"

We rounded the granite-curbed bends of 127, the ocean to our right the entire way. Several of the homes on the way to the quarries were built from huge blocks of granite, con-taining quartz, feldspar, and mica, all visible to the naked eye, as Fred once showed me. Even the base of the Statue of Liberty was made of granite mined from Cape Ann quarries.

We veered off 127, away from the ocean, and drove to the edge of the woods.

"I can't see anything," Fred moaned, looking out the window as the car stopped.

Bridget unclicked her seat belt and turned around. "Freddy, try to have a good time."

"He didn't ask to be here," Fiona said.

"What's your problem?" Bridget asked.

"Nothing," Fiona whispered, leaning her head back on the seat. Dominick popped the trunk and was already out-side the car as another set of headlights came up the road. A Bronco pulled in behind us, blaring ridiculously loud music. It was Lester, Sookie's deckhand.

Lester was built like an ox, which made him look more like a man than the high school kid he still was. Sometimes he sat next to Fred and me on the couch, and we'd watch the Red Sox while Fred's sisters got ready upstairs. Lester was all right, but he wasn't alone in the truck.

Out the back window, Fiona watched Simon Cabot climb down from the passenger's seat, and she straightened her back. Simon was a tall, blond boy who went to boarding school at St. Mark's, which could have been in the Dominican Republic for all we knew. He returned to Rockport for holidays and summer vacations.

"How many people are coming?" Fred asked, leaning over me to peer out his sister's window.

Bridget had already left the car, and Fiona gave Simon a small wave and a restrained smile. It was kind of awkward. No one was paying attention to Fred, and I didn't have an answer for him.

We cleared out of the back seat of Dominick's car and started off down a short wooded path that Fred and I walked a hundred times in daylight, but never crossed in the dark. We couldn't see a thing, but Dominick had taken a flashlight from his glovebox and Lester had a spotlight, so we took small steps to avoid tripping on any roots or rocks and followed the small beam. There was a damp smell of wet forest and fishy ocean. I heard a clanging of glass bottles in someone's bag.

Puff.

At the end of the path was a huge, rectangular hole in the earth that seemed about a half mile around. Mr. Patterson had told me that over a hundred years ago, laborers had harvested the granite guts of the quarry to build a bridge between Boston and Cambridge. The quarry filled with rainwater, becoming a swimming hole.

There was a crescent moon, which barely threw any light on the surface of the water. Lester's spotlight blazed from the top of a small, flat rock, but cast only a small arc over the ledge of the quarry, out into the water.

"Whoo-hoo!" Lester bolted out from the right and flew into the water, making a splash like an anvil hurled over the side. "It's July," he yelled. "Why is it still so friggin' cold?"

"Incoming!" Dominick yelled from the dark before running into the spotlight and turning to face us as he backflipped into the quarry.

"I never want to see that again," Fred said to me in a monotone, which made me laugh.

Simon appeared next. He entered the water like an Olympic diver. The boys started splashing and lunging at one another. They held each other underwater in the deep reservoir. I couldn't understand why it didn't seem to freak them out.

And then Bridget came into the light, shrieking, covering her chest with one arm and holding her nose with her opposite hand. She plunged into the quarry and resurfaced, spitting and slicking her hair back, all that work down the drain as makeup and hair gel dissolved into the stagnant water. She kept wiping under her eyes.

"It's too quiet," Lester yelled.

There was another splash. I turned to see Fiona's head surface, while she yelled, "It's cold!"

"Have you had enough yet?" I whispered to him, but there was no answer. "Fred?"

Puff.

He reached for my hand. Goose bumps covered my back like a cape. We stood there watching the others.

o o º o

When most of the kids had toweled off and redressed, we sat on blankets and the older kids passed around bottles of Boone's Farm, Wild Turkey, and Colt 45. Lester placed the spotlight at the base of a tree nearby. Simon was still floating around in the quarry.

The Boone's bottle came closer. Fiona took a drink and leaned into the circle, so she could skip over Fred and me, to pass the wine to Bridget. Fred intercepted the bottle. Fiona held on to it, looking at Fred, confused. He took the bottle and tipped it to his lips, drinking the pink wine.

"Freddy, take it easy," Bridget said.

"You're too young," Fiona added.

Fred looked at Fiona. "So are you."

And then Fred passed the bottle to me.

I looked at him, as if to say, *What am I supposed to do with this?*

He shrugged.

I had a flashback to fifth grade, when Officer Parrelli came to health class as a guest speaker. I remember role-playing what you're supposed to say if someone offers you a drink and you feel like you're in over your head. But in every scenario at school, it had been a fifth grader, who'd been pretending to be a bully, that had tried to get me to drink. It was never a group of people I loved who were handing me pink wine that smelled like fruit.

I swallowed a mouthful of Boone's, which tasted like carbonated Smarties.

Simon climbed out of the water and dried himself in the darkness before dressing and joining the group. "The quarry freaks me out," he said.

Fiona wrapped a towel around her shoulders. "At least there are no sharks."

I nodded.

"What could Sookie do with the dead great white any-way?" Fiona asked. "Why would he drag it all the way home?"

"He could've sold the teeth or the jaws," Fred said.

"Sookie would've kept the jaws for himself," said Lester. This was probably true.

"Or he could've called a biologist to dissect it," I said.

Fiona nodded. I knew she was thinking of my mom too.

"What would a biologist look for?" asked Bridget.

"I'm not sure yet," I said.

o o º o

An hour or so later, Fred's head was in my lap. We were stargazing, except that whenever I tipped my face back to look up at the sky, I felt dizzy. When I leaned forward, I could smell alcohol and breath, but couldn't distinguish his from mine. Fred was giggling from the story he had told five minutes ago about the time I walked halfway to Gloucester with the back of my skirt tucked into the waistband of my underwear.

"When was the last time you wore a skirt?" he asked me.

"Two years ago."

"Do you miss it?"

"Not at all."

Then with the grace of a windup robot, he shifted position, cupped his hand behind my head, and kissed me. The kiss itself was neither dry nor sloppy. Surprised, I stayed there with my mouth pressing against his mouth. Fred's lips felt warm. A current began radiating through my legs. My whole body relaxed like someone was rubbing the bottoms of my feet. I kissed him back, until the dizziness returned.

Our faces broke apart. I thought I might be sick. Immediately I stood up, forcing Fred to move away. I needed to find my sea legs. My foot pressed into Fiona's hand, as she and Simon carried on a conversation. She was so enraptured that she didn't flinch.

Fred jumped up and followed me.

"Are you okay?" he asked, his eyes darting around, trying to read my face. "Was that okay?"

"Yeah, it was okay. Weird, but okay." I smiled.

"Weird?" he repeated.

"Yeah," I said. "But I like weird."

He smiled and I saw all of his teeth.

"One last time!" Lester announced. Stripping off his shirt, he jumped from the ledge.

I watched Fred as he saw Lester plunge into the quarry.

"Let's go," Fred said.

"Swimming?"

He nodded.

I shook my head. "I've had enough weird tonight. I'm good."

"No, c'mon," he said. "The stars."

He pointed to the sky over the giant hole in the earth. The clouds were breaking like a roof opening above our heads.

"I'm gonna go," he said, pulling off his sweatshirt. "Come swimming if you want."

He smiled again and jumped off the ledge in his shorts. I watched the spot in the water where he entered the quarry until he rose up and his head broke through.

The next thing I knew, Fiona jumped in, followed by Simon, Bridget, and Dominick. I watched everyone from the overhang. I took off my sweatshirt, but I couldn't bear to remove anything else. It felt wrong to be with these older kids. There was only four years' difference between Fiona and me, but it felt like an enormous divide, like a whole canyon with Fred and me on one side and the rest of the group on the other.

I stood on the ledge, wondering if I had really just kissed Fred. He called to me from the water below.

I jumped from the rock into the cold water. I wasn't afraid. A cocoon of bubbles spun around my body as I plunged down and bobbed back up to the surface, my T-shirt ballooning away from my chest. When I wiped the hair out of my face, I began treading water.

In the daylight, the water was clear enough to see fathoms beneath the surface. This gave the illusion there was a bottom that might be safely reached, when really the quarry was so deep even a strong swimmer should consider it bottomless. At night, it was a different story. Since the light beams from Lester's spotlight didn't shine directly down into the water, the quarry seemed black, with unending depth. I could see Lester's head bobbing.

Bridget and Fiona splashed each other before attacking Simon.

I stopped thinking about the darkness and depth when I looked up into the night sky. There were millions of stars surrounding the crescent moon. Bluish Vega, Cassiopeia. Ursa Major.

"Fred," I yelled. "Meteorites."

They were tiny white lights zooming behind black curtains in the sky. I could feel the water covering my ears so that I heard nothing but the blood in my head pulsing and saw nothing but pinpricks of light above.

"Fred?" I called.

He never answered.

14. *The Golden Hour*

WHEN A CHILD IS LOST AT THE BOTTOM OF A QUARRY, EVERY minute counts. Dad had told me this plenty of times before. The *primary diver* enters the water tethered to a search line as tall as a skyscraper. The *line tender* holds the line above the surface. The primary diver descends through the dark and cold until he hits bottom, stirring up a thick cloud of silt and sediment. It is so dark that even with a searchlight nothing would be visible. Touch is the only useful sense. He gives a tug on the line to let the line tender know he has reached bottom.

The line tender holds the line and directs the diver in an *arch search*, the primary diver moving in a three-foot circle around himself, feeling for the child. If the primary diver does not find him, he goes out another three feet and searches that field. And so on, making larger circles on the quarry floor.

After twenty minutes with no sign of the child, the primary diver would have to resurface. The pressure and cold at that depth is dangerous. The *safety diver* takes the primary diver's place while the primary diver rests.

The divers would hope to find the child within sixty minutes, a time span known as the golden hour. The child's heart rate slows. His blood stops flowing to his fingers and toes, his hands and feet, his arms and legs, to conserve blood for the heart and brain. Children are particularly resilient when submerged in cold water.

On the surface, the line tender, the family, the police, and the paramedics wait for four tugs on the line. Four tugs from the bottom of the quarry signal that the child is found. Six tugs signals an emergency. Everyone prepares to take him from the water, wrap him in blankets, give him rescue breaths and chest compressions, all while they bring him to the ambulance. They don't quit until he is either conscious or pronounced dead at the hospital.

Fred was pronounced at 11:52 p.m.

15. *In Our Best Clothes*

DAD AND I SAT NEAR THE FRONT OF THE CHURCH, BESIDE the Station of the Cross, *Jesus meets his mother*. Mr. Patterson was to my right. People fanned themselves with programs in the July heat while the organist plodded out hymns. Every seat was taken.

Like most churches on the North Shore, this one suffered from a lack of air-conditioning and we were all sweating in our best clothes. There were two giant fans at the front of the church, one by the tabernacle and one next to the statue of Saint Joseph. It was like sitting on a tarmac instead of in a sanctuary. I could barely hear, as if my ears were still full of water.

When my mom was alive, I'd gone to church more often. She'd told me once that she didn't believe that any one religion was doing it right, but that she was open to the fact that there might be a higher power. Sometimes she'd felt it at church, sometimes she'd felt it on the ocean. She and I didn't go to church every Sunday, but we used to go to mass outside of Easter and Christmas. Dad would come with us occasionally, but after she died, we started skipping even some of the holidays. When I sat in the pews, I remembered the times that Mom and I came here together, but I bet Dad mostly thought about her funeral.

Dad sat with his right leg sticking out into the aisle, a hard cast wrapped around his foot like a cement boot. Under the pew, I tapped his metal crutches with the tip of my blue canvas shoe. He was one of the rescue divers called to the quarry to find Fred. In the darkness and rugged terrain of the quarry bottom, Dad's foot was crushed by a tree limb. Six tugs to the line tender.

I looked at Mr. Patterson beside me. He was wiping his eyes with a handkerchief. I don't remember many details from my mom's funeral, but I do remember how sad Mr. Patterson was that day. He sat up front with Dad and me, like he was Mom's father. He had outlived all of my biological grandparents, and he had owned the house across the street from my mom since she was a baby. My dad held Mr. Patterson's glasses, so that he could wipe the tears from his whole face.

"The Pattersons didn't have kids of their own," Dad had told me later that night. "So she was theirs too."

"You doing okay?" Mr. Patterson asked, putting his handkerchief in his lap.

I nodded.

Maggie Kelly looked as small as a child, propped up between Fiona and Bridget. My eyes filled and I pulled a Kleenex from the pocket of my navy-blue dress. I hated seeing Maggie like that. When Mom died, Maggie drew a direct line to me. She fed me. She picked me up from school. She asked me if my homework was in my bag. I watched her, pressed into Fiona's side, and I blew my nose into the tissue. Fred's dad sat next to Bridget. I hadn't seen him in a few weeks.

Fred's casket remained at the end of the long aisle in front of us, under a large, white cloth. The casket had been closed at the wake, and I let myself think that maybe he wasn't in there at all. That he somehow escaped the quarry and was only missing.

I suddenly felt hot and sick like someone was pounding a glowing forge in my gut. I started gagging on my own saliva. Unable to make a sound, I slapped Dad's arm. When he saw the panic in my face, he said, "Go get some air at the back of the church. I'll be right behind you."

He flattened his back to the oak pew, so I could climb over him, and I hustled down the aisle to the back of the church. Since the accident, I had trouble swallowing, and the more I thought about it, the worse it was. I focused on the light coming through the open doors, trying not to look at any faces, while I flew down the aisle like a lunatic. By the time I got near the end, I could hear the clicks of Dad's crutches, as he began his long journey to the back of the church.

"How are you now?" Dad asked, breathless. I didn't hear the words over the fan and the priest's voice, but I read his lips. Sweat ran down his cheeks from his sideburns.

"Okay. Can we just stay here?"

Dad nodded. One of the ushers brought him a chair.

"It happened again," I said, looking down at Dad.

"I noticed."

"When's it going to stop?"

He shrugged. "Hopefully soon."

In the ambulance at the quarry, the paramedic had said the choking feeling was probably my brain's response to the accident. That for a while, I might feel panic even when I was in no danger. In the back of the ambulance, with Fiona, I had tried to imagine a string that wrapped around my hand. It had threaded out the door of the truck. It had crossed the dirt path and avoided the feet of those watching the rescue efforts, draping over the cliff. It had dropped into the water, the end of the string moving toward Fred like there was a gravitational pull. And when it found him, the string curled around Fred's wrist. I held the line.

o o º o

In the back of the church, I stood beside my dad, spitting saliva into a Kleenex. I couldn't swallow.

The deacon walked up to the lectern to give a reading.

Dad squeezed my free hand. I remembered standing with Fred on the quarry ledge.

In the pews I saw more kids than I'd ever seen in church. A half a dozen from the chess team were sitting together. Fred liked those guys, though he could beat them all. There were dozens more who didn't give him the time of day. Some of them were crying too.

I saw Sookie sitting beside Paulie. Officer Parrelli was out of uniform, but his clothes were perfectly ironed. Dad's dive team took up two rows. The phone had rung many times since the accident and almost every time I asked him who was calling, it turned out to be one of the guys on the team. My dad ignored most of the calls.

People in the pews were starting to move toward the aisle and I didn't want to talk to anyone.

"I need to go outside," I said.

"I'll wait for Mr. Patterson," he said. "But I'll be there soon."

I walked into the bright sunlight and heat, looking for a place to hide before ducking under a dwarf tree beside the church entrance. The mourners started coming out. I watched Mrs. Lynch, from the bookstore, come down the steps alone. She looked tired. Fred was one of her regular customers. A man from the funeral home opened up the back of the hearse and hurried into the church against the flow. And then I saw our science teacher, Ms. Solomon, come out. She was sobbing, like she had held it in until she walked out the door. Her husband was a builder, and I'd never seen him in a suit before. He held his hand on her back as they walked down the steps.

He whispered something to her and squeezed her arm. Then, he picked up his pace and headed for the sidewalk.

Ms. Solomon pulled another tissue out of her pocket, blew her nose loudly, and made a grunting sound. Watching her cry made tears spill down my cheeks again. She began walking toward my tree, and my heart started beating quickly. Had she seen me? What was I supposed to say? I just wanted to be alone.

And then she caught my eyes.

She sucked in a loud breath and walked over, stopping a foot in front of me. We were almost the same height now. Ms. Solomon had freckles like mine, and short dark hair. She wore comfortable, baggy clothes, even at a funeral. She took another step forward and hugged me with her whole body. I'm pretty sure I got snot on her shoulder.

I had a history of being difficult in Ms. Solomon's class. Like the time when she wanted us to act out the mathematical equation for photosynthesis and I rolled my eyes at her when I thought she wasn't looking.

She had said, "Did you just roll your eyes at me?"

And I said, "No, I was trying to clean my contacts. I swear."

Except, I've never worn contacts.

But here I was, hugging Ms. Solomon, in the heat, under a tree.

"How are you?" she asked.

"I'm okay."

Her dangly feather earrings tickled my neck.

We broke apart and she wiped under her eyes with the backs of her hands.

It was Fred who had proposed the field guide to Ms. Solomon during the last week of school. Ms. Solomon wasn't used to her students assigning themselves homework over the summer. I was surprised when she suggested that I help. To tell the truth, I had just wanted to hang out with Fred and I didn't think we'd get very far anyway. Maybe I'd been right.

A car idled on the street in front of the church. Ms. Solomon turned her head toward the sound.

"You ready?" her husband called from the car window.

She grabbed my hand and said, "Call me at home if you need anything."

It was hard to imagine ever picking up the phone to call Ms. Solomon. Fred and my dad were the only people I ever called.

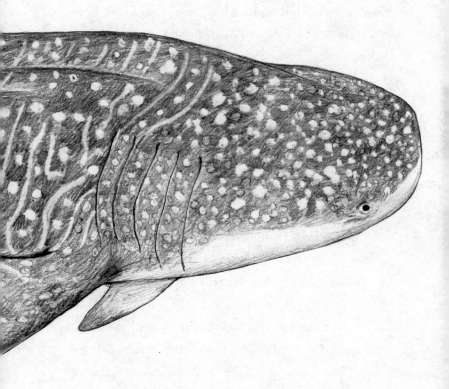

16. *Out the Window*

AFTER THE FUNERAL, I DIDN'T GO OUTSIDE FOR A COUPLE of days. I mostly stayed in my room and watched the Sox downstairs at night. I kept an eye on Fred's house from the window. Mostly visitors went in and came out shortly after.

On account of his foot, Dad was pretty much living on the couch. One morning, I ventured downstairs and he had made his way into the kitchen and was sitting at the table, with his foot on a chair. We were on the same schedule: forage, nap, Red Sox, insomnia. It was unclear when he'd be able to go back to work, but he couldn't drive for at least another five weeks.

I gave the sports page to my dad and unfolded the metro region section. The day after the accident I began to piece together what happened at the quarry, trying to pull out the details that my father wouldn't give me. After Fred went under and Bridget helped me out of the water, I spent the rest of the search under a blanket with Fiona, then inside the back of an ambulance. It was as if everyone was trying to keep me away from the scene.

I read the *Gloucester Daily Times* and the *Boston*

Globe every day. The *Globe*'s articles about the accident were short. I didn't understand how Fred's death could be reduced to a blurb. The *Gloucester Times* provided more details.

The paper explained that a group of teenagers were swimming in the quarry after dark. A thirteen-year-old boy had gone missing in the water.

The way I had imagined the search effort was accurate, but each article had a small detail that grounded the incident, yet made it seem impossible that I had experienced the same accident. Most of the articles disagreed on the depth at which Fred was found.

Monday's *Times* quoted Sergeant Jalbert as saying the dive team untangled Fred from tree limbs. Tuesday's *Times* included that "a family friend, Tom Everhart" was the diver to actually locate Fred. When I read the words, my heart stopped. My dad sat quietly beside me, eating cereal.

"*You* found Fred?" I asked.

"Yeah," he said.

"Why didn't you tell me?"

He shrugged. "I didn't want to upset you."

This might have been true. But I knew Dad. Sometimes he didn't like to talk about the things I wanted to talk about the most.

That particular morning was Wednesday, and the papers reported another source of blame for the event. A new character appeared in the story, Essex County DA, Michael

Murphy. His quote read that area officials suspected alcohol was a factor in the drowning of the thirteen-year-old.

My stomach flipped.

Dad dropped the Opinion section on the table and made a noise like he couldn't believe what he'd just read.

"What?" I said.

"Nothing," he said.

I picked up one side of the section. He grabbed the other end. The paper was stretched tight between us, like two stubborn dogs who refused to let go of a dirty sock. We stared at each other for a second before I looked down at the headline.

"*Absentee parents, tragic consequences*," I read out loud. "What's that supposed to mean?"

"Don't read it," he said. "He doesn't know what he's talking about."

But I gave the paper a tug and it came free, as if Dad had already given up. It was a letter to the editor from one of the ushers at church.

Last week, a boy died in a Rockport quarry. A thirteen-year-old boy. Statistically, it's young adults who are most likely to die in a quarry accident. Blame it on a lack of judgment from thrill-seeking teenagers who walk around with a superhuman feeling that nothing bad is going to happen. It's all the more reason for parents to keep a close watch on their children. Yet who was looking out for Fred Kelly the night that he died?

"Why would he say that?" My voice cracked. "He *knows* Maggie."

Dad put his hand over mine and looked me in the eye. "He's a nut."

"No, but WHY?" I asked Dad again.

I could tell that he was searching for the right words, but he was struggling.

"Sometimes it's easier for people to make sense of things . . . if they can put the blame on someone."

"But why?"

He shook his head.

I heard Maggie's voice in my head, barking at Fred about his inhaler. I put my face in my hands.

There was a knock at the back door and whoever it was didn't wait for my dad to let him in before opening the screen door.

"There they are," Mr. Patterson said, walking into the kitchen from the mudroom. "How are you both feeling?"

"Fine," I said. "Horrible."

On the night of the accident, while Dad was having X-rays, Mr. Patterson sat beside me in the waiting room. I wanted to thank him, but I didn't know what to say.

Mr. Patterson sat down at the table, and Dad offered him a cup of coffee.

"Why don't you go next door? Go check up on Maggie or the young girl," said Mr. P.

"Fiona?"

"Maybe you could use each other is all," he said.

I didn't know what to say. I just hoped Maggie hadn't read today's paper.

"If there's anything I can do, Lucy," said Mr. Patterson. "You know where to find me, dear."

"Thanks," I said. "I'm going to go upstairs for a bit."

And I stayed there all day, except to check on Dad a couple of times.

o o º o

Later that night, I was still sitting up in my room. Out the window, I heard boys' voices coming closer as they whizzed by on bikes. I rested my elbows on the windowsill and knelt on the rug, watching as the two kids pedaled past the gazebo. I wondered where they were going, what they were up to. I stared at Fred's house across the narrow street, wishing he would open his window.

And then his light went on.

For a second I let myself believe that he was home. The shades were up, curtains wide-open. I could see the Zeppelin poster of clasperless Icarus hanging over his bed and the framed picture of Richard Feynman on the wall. I heard Fred's voice in my head, *"He won the Nobel Prize AND he could play the bongos."*

"Whatever! He helped create the A-bomb, for chrissakes," I had said.

Then I saw Maggie. She stood in the bright room, staring at the artifacts the way I stared at Feynman. She sat down on Fred's unmade bed, grabbed a sweatshirt down by the foot, and buried her face in it. I assumed she was crying, but when she brought the cloth down to her lap, she just looked pale. Maggie, Fred, and I all had Irish skin that turned red just before we cried. Maggie was still white. Then she did it again, but this time when the sweatshirt dropped below her nose, she saw me across the narrow street, watching her from my own room.

My heart was beating triple time, but then I waved at her involuntarily, like I was brushing away a bee. She got up and opened the window.

"Hi," Maggie said across Smith Street.

"Hi."

We just stared at each other.

"You want to come over?" she asked.

"Sure," I said.

"I'm going to Fred's," I yelled, closing the front door. I didn't realize how weird it sounded until it was already out there, but I kept walking.

o o ° o

Maggie met me at the front door wearing a Rockport High School T-shirt that looked like it had belonged to Fred's dad and a pair of shorts that showed 98 percent of her compact legs. She looked top heavy. We both studied each other's face. Maggie's brow furrowed.

She hooked me around the back with her arm and pressed my head into her hair. Maggie raised her face to kiss my cheek, and I bawled all over her. Her breath smelled like booze.

"You doing okay?" she asked.

"Not really."

"Me either. Let's go upstairs."

Wiping my eyes, I looked down the hall into the kitchen and wondered if Bridget and Fiona were home.

"I'll go get some more Kleenex," Maggie said. The light was still on in Fred's room. It was hard to tell if anything had been touched. Fred was meticulous. All of his books were on the shelves. The drafting table was bare except for a blotter and a Sox mug full of mechanical pencils. His postcard of Miles Davis wearing the bug-eyed glasses was pinned to the bulletin board above his desk. Fred's music was tucked away in a storage case, except for a smaller case on top of the stereo that held maybe a dozen CDs. It looked like a small, square book, except the cover was an old Massachusetts license plate. This was where he kept the music he wanted to listen to most.

His laundry sat in the hamper, except the sweatshirt Maggie had draped over the foot of the bed. But the unzipped backpack, leaning against the leg of a desk chair—and the sheets, balled in the middle of the mattress—made me feel like he was alive. Fred was not a bed-maker. A fresh glass was sweating all over the bedside table—something with ice and brown liquid.

I spied Fred's inhaler and the bug-eyed glasses on the bedside, and for the first time in my life—though I'd always been curious—I picked up the inhaler and gave myself a puff the way I had seen him do a thousand times. With a swift kick, my heart started racing, and just as I returned the inhaler to the table, Maggie appeared in the doorway.

With jittery fingers, I blew my nose into a Kleenex and sat on the bed, careful not to disturb the disturbed sheets. Maggie sat in the chair. She handed me the sweatshirt and grabbed her drink.

"Smell it," she said, flicking her index finger toward the sweatshirt.

I looked at her.

"Smell it."

I sniffed back the mucus in my nose, like I was clearing my palate, and put the sweatshirt up to my face. It smelled like nothing. Like cotton.

I shook my head. "It doesn't smell like anything."

Her nose started blooming red, so I put my face back into the thick fabric and tried again. Maybe detergent, maybe deodorant. Fred wasn't great about remembering to slick up his pits in the morning. Still, it didn't smell like sweat, either.

"You want it to smell like Fred?"

She nodded.

"I don't smell him," I said.

"That's what I thought."

"I wish I did," I said.

She breathed in heavy through her nose and gave me a flat smile. Her ankle started twitching and her bare toes tapped the carpet. "How's your dad?"

"He's doing okay," I said. "Has to wear the cast for six weeks."

"I've been meaning to check up on him." She sighed. "What have you been up to?"

"Not much." I put down the sweatshirt.

Maggie looked into her glass. "I'm so sorry I sent you and Fred to look after Bridget and Fi that night. That was wrong."

I didn't know how to respond, so I just nodded.

"I thought you were just gonna watch a movie and come home."

She took the last sip of her drink. "I thought Dominick was the one I had to worry about." Her ankle twitched faster. "Not Lester."

"What?" But as soon as I spoke, I understood her accusation. I no longer thought she might cry. Her eyes looked like a wolf's.

"I was counting on Lester to be more of an adult."

Her tone made me hope that we weren't alone in the house, which is something I had never felt before with Maggie. Her face was red and it looked like she could spring out of the chair.

"I don't know who brought the alcohol. And nobody forced us to drink it," I said.

"You don't give booze to a couple of kids and let 'em go in the water. Especially when you're studying to be a paramedic."

She stood up and took a lap around her chair. I felt terrified. There was a knock on the open door. Fiona leaned against the molding.

"Hey," she said softly, eyeing her mother.

Fiona crept into the room and sat down beside me on the bed, her left shoulder gently bumping my right shoulder from behind. I hoped she would stay close like that, but Maggie barked, "Don't mess up the sheets!" And Fiona slid off the bed, onto the carpet.

I hadn't seen her since the funeral. Fiona's hair was sticking up on the right side of her head like she'd been sleeping. She looked like she could use another eight hours. And I hadn't seen her with bare lips since she was my age. For some reason I started picking and flattening her cowlicks with my fingers like we were a couple of gorillas.

"Dad said for you to call," Fiona said.

"What does he want?" Maggie asked.

"I don't know."

"For *Jay*sus' sake," she said, putting her empty glass on the drafting-table blotter. I expected it to roll off into the open backpack, but it stayed in place. Maggie left the room.

"Don't stop," Fiona added, resting her head on my

knee. I continued separating and smoothing pieces of her pixie haircut. She looked boyish with messed-up hair and no makeup.

I slid off the bed and sat beside her.

"You okay?"

"What do you think? How are *you*?"

I shook my head. She nodded.

"Where's Bridget?"

"Staying at a friend's. Probably at Dominick's. My mom hates him even more now."

"She's really angry," I said. Fiona nodded.

"I'm so tired," she finally said. "Every time I try to sleep I start thinking about horrible things. Seeing Freddy. The cops and divers who kept pushing Bridget and my mom away. Reporters."

"You saw Fred?"

"Just a flash. When I left you in the ambulance to check on my mom. The paramedics brought him by on a board, wrapped up in blankets. They hadn't given up on him yet, but he was dead. So pale. Paler than usual. And his face was scratched."

I couldn't swallow and I almost got up to run to the bathroom. I must have looked like I was choking because Fiona said, "You all right?"

I nodded, working down the saliva. My heart was racing.

"Lucy, I'm sorry."

"I really feel like I'm going to throw up," I said, leaning

my head back on the bed. Fiona took my hand and started pinching my palm between the thumb and index finger.

"What are you doing?"

"I don't know. One of these pressure points is supposed to help."

"I forgot about puking because my hand hurts like hell."

"Just don't barf in here. My mom will go nuts."

"I'll try not to."

"You must miss him like crazy," she said.

"I do," I said.

Fiona kept squeezing my skin and muscle.

"You mind if I ask you something?" she asked.

"Go ahead."

"I saw him kiss you that night. I thought you were *friends*," she said.

"We are." *Were.*

"Were you something else too?"

"You mean like boyfriend-girlfriend?"

"Yeah."

"No. I mean, I don't know."

She stopped pinching my pressure points and held my hand.

"I suppose Maggie would be upset if I brought a few things home, from Fred's room, I mean."

"What do *you* think?"

I shrugged.

"What do you want?" Fiona asked.

"The field guide and my mom's research proposal. They're in the backpack."

Fiona stood up and walked to the window. She pinched the tabs and pushed the screen up. "Get the backpack," she said. "Hurry."

"What are you doing?"

"My mom isn't going to let anyone walk out of this house with anything that belonged to Fred. Not yet. And not even you," she said. "You can pick them up on your way home. *Hurry.*"

I picked up the backpack, but before I could hand it off, I looked at the license plate CD case and stuffed it into the bag. I passed the backpack to Fiona. She tossed it out the window.

"Really, Fiona?" I said.

"Go pick it up," she said. "Before Mom goes out there."

Now that the backpack was lying in the grass, I had a sudden urge to run outside and grab it.

We heard Maggie's feet on the steps.

Maggie entered the room again, just as Fiona clicked the screen tabs shut.

"What are you doing at the window?" Maggie sniffed the air.

"Letting a spider out," Fiona answered.

"Just kill it next time," Maggie said, picking up the empty glass.

I looked at Fiona.

"Thanks for inviting me over, Maggie," I said. "It was good to see you."

"Anytime, dear. Say hi to your dad."

I nodded, then looked at Fiona. "Thanks for the talk, Fi."

"You too," she said. By her face, I thought she was sad to see me go.

I busted out of the house to scoop up the backpack.

17. *Fred's Backpack*

ONCE IN THE HOUSE, I SAT AT THE FOOT OF THE STAIRS AND unzipped Fred's backpack, the smell of cinnamon gum leaking into the air. It felt a little weird to be looking in his bag, even though he wasn't there to complain.

I pulled out the field guide with its blue canvas cover and leafed through the pages. Everything was printed in Fred's tiny, precise handwriting. His penmanship was a sure indicator that he would have had a future at MIT, the minuscule mechanical pencil marks designed to maximize the amount of cryptic data a genius could record on one page.

I grabbed a yellow legal pad where Fred had recorded pages of notes on great white shark behavior, reproduction, and something called *osmoregulation*. In the behavior section, Fred wrote "spy-hopping" and drew a trio of stars in the left margin that caught my eye.

Spy-hopping—Great whites, one of a few shark species to regularly lift their heads above the surface to seek prey!

I liked his exclamation point. The idea of spy-hopping was creepy because it was so human and calculated. I imagined a shark popping her head above water, getting a look at a colony of fat, tasty seals sunning themselves on the rocks. Then she'd slip below the surface, swim nearer, and attack them from beneath.

I did not speak the language of biology or understand the characteristics that grouped one shark with another. But I liked the behavioral anecdotes. So I kept reading about shark embryos that snack on their lesser sisters and eventually devour other siblings in the womb until the fittest shark remains and the mother gives birth to only one baby. Freaky.

I skimmed pages of notes about how great whites breathe, digest, and reproduce, stopping every once in a while when Fred included a thought followed by exclamation points like, *No one has ever seen a white shark mate!!*

I put the legal pad on the step beside me and slipped my mom's research proposal out of the backpack.

PROPOSAL FOR CAPE COD WHITE SHARK AND GRAY SEAL STUDY

I smoothed my palm over the cover, flattening a corner that might have bent in the fall from Fred's window. The date and her name were typed in the lower-right-hand corner, along with someone else's name.

Helen Everhart. That was my mom.

But there was a name below hers. *Vernon Devine.*

I ran my finger over Vernon Devine.

I could hear my dad banging jars around in the refrigerator. I set the proposal on top of the legal pad on the stairs and walked into the kitchen.

My dad was sticking out of the open fridge, balancing on one crutch.

"Want some pie?" he asked, backing out of the refrigerator with a glass dish. It was blueberry with a golden crust.

"Where did that come from?"

"Someone from work brought it by today."

I pulled down the plates from the cabinet and grabbed a couple of forks from the drawer. Dad poured two glasses of milk and we sat at the table.

"How did it go across the street?" he asked.

"Really weird," I said. I was going to leave it alone, but he kept looking at me like he was waiting for me to elaborate. "Maggie is a mess. Fiona is afraid of her. I almost threw up in Fred's room."

I took a small bite of the blueberry pie and chewed carefully. But when it came time to swallow, I panicked and reached for the milk, taking large sips to wash down the pie. I pushed the plate aside. Dad had his foot up on a chair and was trying to scratch an itch inside of his cast with a chopstick.

"How long until you can dive again?" I asked.

My father put the chopstick down. He rested his elbow on the table and cupped his chin in his hand.

"By winter," he said. "We'll see."

"You really haven't talked too much about what happened."

He rubbed his face. In another couple of days, his stubble would be a beard. "Lucy, I don't want you to hear all that stuff. It's better for you that way."

"I want to know," I said.

He wiped his mouth with a napkin and breathed out. He thought for a moment.

"Lester and Bridget showed us where Fred went under. But when we went down, we came up on a mess of debris. Mostly tree limbs. That stuff can hook your tanks and hoses. The line tender was concerned about the divers' safety."

"Were you afraid?"

"No. The captain went down to inspect the area. We'd already passed the end of the golden hour. But everyone holds out hope anyway.

"I thought we'd wasted so much time. I just started to lose it. I felt like I was looking for my own kid."

My throat was starting to close up again. I felt panicky and grabbed the milk. My dad didn't notice anything. He was looking down at the half-eaten pie.

"I couldn't see anything down there. Not even with a light," he said. "And there was Fred, in a precarious spot. I should've gone at it a different way, but I moved some debris so I could get to him, and a log came down on my foot. And all I could think about was getting him up."

"I'm sorry you got hurt," I said.

"No," he said. "I shouldn't have gotten in the water at all because it was Fred. It's personal. But I never would have stayed out of the quarry. I thought I could bring him back."

I put my elbows up on the table, dropped my face into my hands, and started to cry. Dad rubbed my back.

We just sat there for a long time.

"Why did you go over to Fred's tonight?" he asked.

"I was looking out the window into Fred's room and Maggie was there. She saw me and told me to come over," I said, stopping to blow my nose on a napkin. "I wanted the field guide back."

I didn't have to explain the field guide to Dad.

"Fiona didn't think Maggie would let me take any-thing of Fred's. So Fiona threw them out the window and I brought them home."

"Maggie knows the field guide is yours. She wouldn't try to keep it."

"Well, she didn't seem like herself, and it was Fiona's idea to make it into a projectile."

"Okay," he said. "What else did Fiona throw out the window?"

"Fred's backpack," I said. "And the last research pro-posal that Mom wrote."

He scratched his left sideburn. "Why did Fred have it?"

"We found it the other day. He wanted to read it, so I let him take it home."

It was quiet for a bit. I could hear a car drive down our street.

"Who was Vernon Devine?" I asked.

He half smiled. "Vern's a shark expert. Kind of like your mom's mentor. Why?"

"His name was on the proposal too."

"They worked on a lot of projects together."

"Was he with her when she died?" I asked.

"Vern? No. He was retired even back then and he didn't go out on research boats much anymore."

I nodded.

Quietly, I headed for the stairs. Fred's backpack sat like a peeled banana on the step. I scooped up the proposal and the legal pad, but when I went to stuff them into the backpack, there was a noise like two metal things colliding. I figured one of them was the license plate CD case, but I dug my hand inside anyway and pulled out a strange package. It was a pathetically gift-wrapped box, the size of a Band-Aid tin. The grandma-like paper was a meadow of watercolor flowers, held together by yards of Scotch tape. It wasn't my birthday. Not even close. It wasn't Maggie Kelly's birthday or Mother's Day. I shook the box a few times. It made a tiny sound, like something soft shifting from top to bottom.

I slung the backpack over my shoulder and carried the package upstairs, closing my bedroom door behind me. I stared at the box, wanting to open it. Technically, it had no owner, which meant that I could claim it for my own. But I didn't want to take away someone else's gift from Fred. I shook it. I smelled it (more cinnamon gum). And then I dropped the backpack and tried to rip it open with two hands.

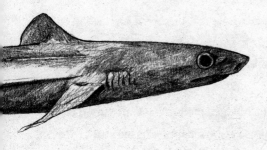

18. *Postcard*

I STARED AT THE HIDEOUS PAPER, MY HEART POUNDING. IT could be something I might actually want, like a silver ring with a moonstone. Or it could be bones and teeth from an owl pellet, which only Fred would have thought was cool. Though the more I thought of Fred this summer, the more I wondered if it could be something I'd never guess.

He must have used a whole roll of tape. I jammed my finger into an open pocket in the seam, wiggled it until the tape split, and the flowery paper fell away like a snake shedding its skin.

It was, in fact, a Band-Aid box, made of tin with a flip-top, that once held a family-size assortment of "Plastic Strips."

"He's resourceful," I whispered, flicking the lid with my thumbnail. *Pop*.

I looked inside. The mystery object was bundled in Kleenex—no, toilet paper. I slid my fingers inside and pulled out the wad. It felt thin and long, weighty. I ruled out *shark's teeth* and *a ring*. I put the tin on the floor, so I could peel away the sheets of tissue. Slowly the object came into focus as the toilet paper became thin and sheer, like I'd adjusted a microscope. A skinny rod of yellow gold. I removed the final ply of tissue to reveal what looked like a crayon dipped in gold with a lanky mermaid swimming the length of the piece.

"What is it?" I whispered to nobody.

There was no chain, but there was a loop on top, as if it were a pendant. I turned it on its side, revealing two clasps, like hinges. It wouldn't open. There was a small hole in the base. I ran a fingertip over the mermaid. The whole thing looked really old.

I took a seat at my desk and surveyed the landscape—a small village of nail polish bottles, colored pencils, a rubber finger-puppet beast, and a hill of assorted notepads. And then I spotted the little plastic container of dental floss—cinnamon, no less. I made a long triple loop and tied a knot at the back of my neck. The mermaid hung below my heart like a pendulum on a grandfather clock. It smelled like Fireballs—another candy Fred and I never bothered with. I wished I knew where it came from and whether it was mine.

I picked up the Band-Aid tin and looked through all of the toilet paper for a note, but there was nothing. Maybe he figured he'd explain it himself or maybe it was not for me.

I wanted to ask him what it all meant.

I opened my desk drawer. Somewhere in there was a stack of postcards from the Museum of Fine Arts in Boston. I bought them on a field trip to decorate the front of my sketchbook and inside my locker. Under an old day planner and a couple of overdue library books, I found the museum gift shop bag.

I brought the stack of cards to my lap, sifting through the images before deciding on a Japanese woodblock print with white foam like snow atop the blue ocean waves. I flipped over the postcard to the side with the box for the stamp and the artist's name. I chose a pen and began to write.

Under the Wave off Kanagawa (ca 1830), Katsushika Hokusai.

I'm pretty sure the snails and whatever else is in your aquarium will die without an intervention, but I don't really want to become a guardian to your orphans. Does that make me a bad person?

Whose gift was that inside your backpack? I hope you don't mind, but I opened it and I claimed the mermaid as my own.

POSTCARD

Fred Kelly

I stared at the final product for a while, wondering what to do next. I found a pair of shoes and I went downstairs. I looked into the living room, where Dad was asleep in front of the Sox game, and slipped out the door, relieved.

I pedaled my bike in the dark to the end of Smith Street, turning onto King, the road that ran into the ocean. The water was a black open space beneath the starry sky. The night air felt clean on my skin and it smelled like wet sand.

It had been a while since I'd been on my bike without Fred. I wobbled into town, as though I had lost muscle memory.

I pedaled to the mailbox at the top of a landing in town, the one that abruptly split the bookstore from an art gallery and offered a sloping alley with a bench at the bottom, a bench with a perfect view of the rocky shoreline. I came to the US mailbox just beyond the bookstore and straddled my bike. I opened the loud metal door before dropping my note into the mailbox. I had no idea where it would land, but I felt lighter inside, as though I had cleared something out of my head.

19. *All Biologists Want to Know Why*

THE NEXT MORNING, I LOOKED FOR STORIES ABOUT THE quarry accident in the *Boston Globe* again. I was getting to the point where I didn't want to read any more details, but I also wasn't ready for Fred's story to dissolve. I worked my way to the metro region section and stopped. It was like when your brain recognizes a snake in the woods before your eyes see it. The story wasn't about Fred. There was a large, grainy image of a body of water and two shapes were at the surface: a long mass like the trunk of a tree, followed by a stubby triangle. I read the caption: KAYAKER TRAILED BY WHITE SHARK OFF CAPE BEACH.

"Holy fish," I whispered, grabbing on to Fred's gold mermaid around my neck.

It was an image of a man in a kayak, looking over his shoulder at a large fin sticking out of the water behind him. I skimmed through the article for the key details. The shark followed the kayak, as the man paddled to shore, but then it swam away—no damage to the boat, no injuries.

White sharks were pretty rare off the coast of Massachusetts. My mom had always said they were there. But up until that summer, I had never heard of a real sighting. Now there had been two in almost as many weeks. That seemed kind of strange. For a second, I had a crazy thought that maybe Fred had sent me the story in the *Globe*, as a response to my postcard. I shook it off.

"Dad?" I yelled.

"What?" he yelled from the couch. "Come here."

I stood in the doorway. "Did you read about the white shark on Cape Cod?" I asked.

"Yeah, I saw that," he said.

"What was Mom's research proposal about?" I asked. "The one that Fiona threw out the window."

He made a half smile. "White sharks on Cape Cod."

"Do you think the kayak shark is connected to Mom's study?"

"Maybe," he said, nodding.

"And Sookie's shark?"

"Maybe."

I ran upstairs, pulled the proposal out of Fred's backpack, and looked down at the cover page.

PROPOSAL FOR CAPE COD WHITE SHARK AND GRAY SEAL STUDY

I opened the proposal, skimmed through the table of contents, and flipped the pages one at a time, trying to make sense of her plan.

The background section explained the idea of the study like a story. The gray seal population off Cape Cod had shrunk because they had been hunted for their meat, oil, and skins. Then, Congress passed a law to stop humans from killing marine mammals. Slowly, the seals had started to return, and Mom and her research partners were watching them.

My mom's interest in the seals was more of an afterthought. She was a shark expert. Fishermen spotted white sharks every once in a while, but they were rare in the waters off Massachusetts. However, it was known that they liked to eat seals, so Mom and her partners thought that if the number of seals off Cape Cod increased enough and the ocean began to warm slightly, the great whites might start coming north. Small seal colonies were starting to form on some of the islands around Nantucket and Cape Cod. Mom had been watching those seal pods for one very large predator.

The next part of the research was a little more confusing to me because of the technical language. From what I understood, mostly from the illustrations, Mom and the researchers wanted to take a harpoon fishing boat into a stretch of Cape Cod where fishermen had spotted white sharks. A harpoon boat has a long catwalk that hangs over the water, so a fisherman can get closer to the big fish. Like Moby Dick close. Mom and the researchers would have to fit the harpoon with an acoustic tag (whatever that was) that would allow them to track the shark. An experienced fisherman would walk to the end of the plank, launching the tag into the shark's dorsal fin. Mom had named a fisherman in the proposal: Paul Sawyer. Sookie.

I walked downstairs and stood in the doorway. Dad was flipping a magazine page.

"What are you up to?" he asked.

"Reading," I said.

"What are you reading?" he asked.

"Mom's study," I said.

He looked up from the page. "That's some light reading," he said.

"It's not bad," I said. "Did the idea of Mom tagging white sharks freak you out?"

"She would have had help," he said. "And I wouldn't have been able to talk her out of it anyway."

"You read the proposal?" I asked.

"Yup."

"So you knew that Sookie was gonna help her?"

"Yup," he said, looking at me sideways, like he wondered where I was going with the question.

"What about Vern?"

"Vern wasn't planning to be on the boat. I think they collaborated on the idea, but your mom was gonna execute it."

He rubbed his face and shook out his dark curls with his hand. "What made you and Fred decide to read Mom's paper?"

"We were looking for books about white sharks to help with the field guide. And Fred found a bunch of her papers on the shelf," I said. "But you know when you go to a bookstore and one book stands out from all of the others? And when you read it, you feel like it picked you?"

"Yup," he said.

"That's it," I said. "Actually, Fred picked it, but I took it from him."

Dad smiled. "What's that around your neck?" he said.

I put my hand to my heart and clutched the gold mermaid. It was cold and heavy.

"Nothing," I said. "I found it."

He looked at me for a moment. "Let me know if you have any questions about Mom's research," he said.

"Okay," I said, stuffing the mermaid into the neck of my shirt. I didn't want to have to explain the pendant to anybody and I didn't want anyone to try to take it away. I took the stairs two at a time and went back to my desk.

I looked down at the research proposal, not ready to tackle the physics of an acoustic tag. I looked out the window across the street. Fred would have been good at figuring out that part.

I closed the cover of the proposal and pulled the postcards from my drawer and I wrote another note to Fred.

Mirror with Minerva, Venus, and Juno,
Roman, Imperial Period (ca AD 100–200).

I got Mom's research proposal back from your house (not easy). Not a bad read so far. ☺ If the seals keep multiplying, how many sharks are we going to get? . . . Did you know that Sookie was going to help Mom tag the sharks? Kinda weird that he would hang over the ocean, tagging sharks in the name of science, but he wouldn't call a biologist to dissect the one he caught, right?

POSTCARD

Fred Kelly
_____
_____
_____

I hopped on my bike and headed into town with the postcard in my back pocket. I thought about the seals that were multiplying off Cape Cod and how if I ever saw them hanging around the beach, I would stay out of the water. Then, I realized that after what I'd been through, it was unlikely I'd be in the water anyway, so I imagined myself warning others. There weren't too many animals on the planet that were capable of eating a human and I had conflicting thoughts about this. On the one hand, I understood the fear that people had about sharks, especially a great white. The possibility of being eaten by a wild animal was a primal fear.

But on the other hand, I thought about what my mom had said in the TV clip. *You just have to remember that you are swimming in their home. You have to know how to behave when you are the guest.*

Humans were guests in the ocean. If white sharks were heading north, what if humans had to adapt?

I dropped the postcard for Fred into the mailbox.

I know you can't write me back, but maybe you could send me a sign.

I looked at the ordinary mailbox and steered my bike back onto the road. I headed straight to Sookie's boat.

o o ° o

Sookie paced around the dock, while Sookie's dad and Lester seemed to be arguing about something. I rode up close to the boat for a better view. It was the first time I'd seen Lester since the accident.

"You're gonna need stitches," Lester said, tugging gauze tightly around Paulie's finger. "You're lucky you didn't lose the whole thing."

"You just do it here."

"No, Paulie. I'll drive you to the hospital," said Lester. "You want to have a doctor do that. In case you got nerve damage or somethin'."

"Why? If it's damaged, it's damaged. What am I gonna do about it? I got things to do," said Paulie.

I was still watching Lester's wrap job, wondering what sort of pulpy mess lay beneath the layers. The blood soaked through as fast as Lester could wind.

Lester taped the end of the gauze and let go of Paulie's hand.

"I think you should see a doctor," I said.

Lester looked up, noticing me for the first time.

"Lucy," Lester said.

I waved.

He walked over to the side of the boat. "How are you doin'?"

I shrugged.

"I miss your buddy," he said. "I'm so sorry."

We looked at each other. My eyes stung.

"I'm bleeding out here!" Paulie said, in an annoyed voice.

"Dad! Go to the hospital!" Sookie said, throwing his gloves across the wet deck.

"Lester's an EMT. That's just as good and he won't bankrupt his parents to pay for med school," Paulie said.

"I think people take out loans for that," I said.

Lester shook his head. "I just started trainin' in June."

"Whatever. Just sew it up," Paulie yelled. "Sook, do we have any Tylenol?"

"You're gonna need more than that, old man," Sookie said, shaking his head.

After several minutes of arguing, Lester opened the passenger-side door of his truck for Paulie, to which Paulie barked, "You ain't my prom date." He slammed the door and opened it again with his good hand.

Once Paulie was safely in his seat, Lester walked in front of the car and grinned at Sookie and me, then rolled his eyes.

"What happened?" I asked as the Bronco pulled away.

"Dad cut his hand on a bait hook. Clear to the bone."

The image of Paulie seeing part of his own skeleton made my stomach bottom out. "Ew," I said.

"You want to help? I'm short a crew," he said.

"What? Me?"

"Sure," said Sookie. "I've some fish to clean."

"On the boat?" I asked.

"Yeah, on the boat," he said.

If he'd asked me the day before, I would have told him he was on his own. He came closer to the side and held up his hand to invite me aboard. I didn't like the green canal between the dock and the *Clara Belle*, but I quit looking down and planted my foot on the side of the boat. Sookie pulled me aboard.

On the boat, he handed me a set of gloves. "Take Lester's."

I slid my hands inside. They were huge.

He passed me a butcher's apron that could have wrapped around my body twice.

"What do you want me to do?" I asked.

He grabbed a fish from a pile of others heaped in a large wooden pen. He threw it onto the counter. With a knife he made a few small cuts above the tail, a couple of clean cuts at the head, and one deep slice up the belly. In a fistful, he yanked out all of the guts, snapped off the tail, and threw the meaty shell into a plastic tote to be weighed and sold. Sookie was all business.

"You try," he said.

He prepared two others before I selected a victim and picked up my knife.

I sawed into the flesh at the tail. "Do you ever get used to the smell?"

"What smell?" he asked.

I looked at him to see if he was joking, but his sun-burned face was expressionless. I thought about how he used to come over our house a lot before Mom died and how it had been a while since I had spent any real time with him. Strange, but it felt normal to be disemboweling fish together.

"Am I doing this right?"

"You're doing fine," Sookie said. "I was thinking about coming to see you and your dad after the funeral. But I didn't know if I should. How's his foot?"

"Broken," I said.

"And how are you?"

"Fine," I said.

He looked me straight in the eye and said, "I'm real sorry about your friend. It's just awful. If there's anything I can do . . ."

His voice trailed off. I knew Sookie was being kind, but there really wasn't anything he could do. I nodded, terrified that I would start bawling on Sookie's boat if I opened my mouth. I looked down at the wet floor and I knew Sookie was still focused on me. It was probably the longest period of time he remained idle on his boat in the history of the *Clara Belle*. Then he grabbed another fish.

"Sookie?" I said, sawing through to the bone.

"What?"

"Remember the day you caught the white shark?"

"Yes, unfortunately."

"Why didn't you call the biologists," I said.

I could tell he wanted to drop the whole thing, but he looked at me and then he said, "I was thinking about it. Like I said, if your mom had been here, I'd have called her right away. But I don't know . . . And then I saw your mom on TV."

My eyes bulged wide.

"And I just lost it." His voice cracked a little. "So I went out with my buddies. And when I came home, I called your mom's old office. Got an answering service. I left a message for them to come in the morning, but by then, it was too late."

Even though everybody watched the local news, I couldn't believe that Sookie had seen Mom too. I wanted to ask him a million questions. *Did you see her smile? Did it feel like she looked at you and only you? Did it make you feel like she was coming home for dinner after the interview?* But I figured Sookie would think I was nuts, so I said, "What made you call the biologists?"

"Because if she were here today, she would have loved to get a crack at that thing," he said.

"Do you have any idea why she liked dissecting sharks?"

He snorted. "I think she was just interested in seeing how different animals were made. She used to get pretty excited when we were out on the boat and we found something new."

"Just like Fred," I said.

"I remember her showing me a squid with three hearts once."

"Why does it need three hearts?"

"Exactly. All biologists want to know why. Just like your mom and Fred," he said, ripping another sack of ugly from the inside of a fish.

"Do you remember why a squid has three hearts?"

"No, but I can tell you how much money squid fetches per pound at the dock." He smiled.

"She was waiting for the white sharks to come. You knew that," I said. "I read her proposal. You were going to help her tag them."

Sookie nodded.

"You ever use a harpoon before?" I asked.

He nodded. "I used to own a harpoon boat. We used it for tuna and swordfish," he said. "I sold it to a buddy of mine, but we had a deal worked out, so I could borrow it back for your mom."

"What's happening with the study now?" I asked.

"Don't know," he said. "A couple of biologists called a few months ago, but I never called back."

Sookie gutted ten fish for every mackerel I threw in the tote.

"Hey, I found something for you." Sookie took off his gloves, went to the wheelhouse, and came back holding an old photograph with faded colors. I looked it over as he pinched it in front of my face.

Dad and Sookie were the bookends with my mom in the middle. She was laughing with a gorgeous mouth and shiny long hair. Sookie wore a huge beard, but my dad looked clean cut, with a short-cropped haircut. He smiled and looked handsome.

"When was that taken?" I asked.

"When we were eighteen."

"Did you have a crush on her?"

"Don't hold back, Lucy!" Sookie snorted. "Everybody wanted to be with your mom. She was smart and funny. And the best part was, she didn't care about any of the boys. I mean, she cared about us, but she wasn't sittin' around waiting for someone to call her. She was always doing somethin' you didn't want any part of. But it made her interesting, you know?"

I understood. I thought about Fred and his filthy aquarium.

"But your mom and dad were meant to be together," he said. "I love them both."

Sookie's brow folded into the center of his face and he looked pained.

"Why don't you and Dad hang out anymore?" I asked.

"I guess we're just busy," he said. He was quiet for a minute. "I guess your mom was always the one to call first, to invite me over for things."

"Are you saying that she liked you more than my dad does?" I asked.

"No. Well, I don't know," he said. "All I am saying is, she was better at reaching out to people than your dad and I are."

I nodded.

"You ever want to come out with me and Lester on the boat?" he asked. "We could use an extra hand."

"I'm not crazy about the water these days," I said. "But thanks."

"Then come down to the dock," he said. "Like today. We'll gut fish."

"That's tempting," I said, looking at the pile of innards. "Maybe. Thanks for the picture."

I stuffed it in my pocket and pedaled away. As I rode home, I felt sorry for Sookie. He had lost both my mom and dad.

When I passed by the taffy pull in the window of the candy store, I thought about calling Fred to see if he wanted to watch the game or hang out. My throat tightened when I realized this was impossible. I stopped the bike and didn't start riding again until I was able to swallow.

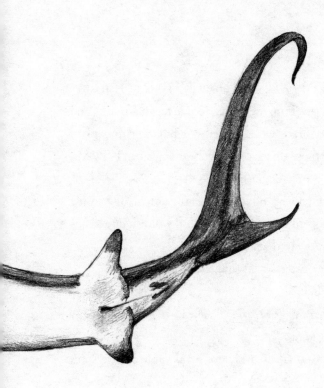

20. *Vern Devine*

I RODE THE REST OF THE WAY HOME IN A FUNK OF FISH GUTS and sweat. I was thinking about Sookie tagging sharks and a squid with three hearts. I needed a biologist to explain how both of those things could work, but instead I saw Mr. Patterson, a retired engineer.

Mr. Patterson was in his chair on the porch. He had fed an extension cord through a crack in the screen door, connected to a box fan that blew at his feet.

"Hey, Mr. Patterson," I said, ascending the steps.

"Hello, Lucy."

"Can I share your breeze?" I asked.

"Go right ahead."

I took a seat on the warm floor planks at Mr. Patterson's feet.

"Neighbors are supposed to check on old people when it's hot outside. To make sure they're okay. You okay?"

"What do you think?" he asked.

"I don't know. I'm just checking."

"It's only eighty-five degrees and we live a block from the ocean. But thanks."

I nodded.

"It's good to see you out and about." He poured a glass

of poop-brown water from a Tupperware pitcher and handed it to me. "Here. You're sweating like a pig."

"Thanks," I said. Lipton iced tea. Sweet but no longer cold. "Do I smell like fish?"

"Like what?"

"Fish. I was working with Sookie."

Mr. Patterson raised his eyebrows. "How did that go?"

"Okay, I think." I took a sip of tea. "Did you know Sookie was going to help my mom with a research project?"

Mr. P shook his head.

"Yeah. She was gonna tag great white sharks," I said. "I've been trying to figure it out, but I think I need to go to grad school first."

"No, you're smart," he said. "You'll make sense of it. What did Sookie have to say about it?"

"Not much," I said. "There was this other guy, Vern Devine. His name is on the front of the proposal."

"Why don't you call him?" Mr. Patterson asked.

"What?" I asked. "No. He lives in Maine and besides, I guess he's really old."

Mr. Patterson looked at me in disbelief.

"Sorry. That's not what I meant," I said.

Mr. Patterson took another sip of tea. "I haven't been to Maine in a long time. Bea and I used to spend a couple of weeks of the summer in South Freeport. I like Maine. All of those pine trees and islands. Not so many people up there."

Mr. Patterson brought the hot iced tea to his lips, his long, liver-spotted fingers gripping the glass. He wore a chunky gold ring and kept neatly trimmed nails. I wondered if it helped his French horn playing to have such long fingers, like a pianist. He cleared his throat and started again.

"We used to take a boat—barely seaworthy—out to French's Island, sit on the beach, and drink Moxie."

I pictured Mr. Patterson and his wife on a scratchy wool blanket at the edge of the tide. At first I imagined them in their seventies and then I guessed what they looked like in their twenties. I put Mr. Patterson in a pair of white shorts with skinny white legs sticking out and I gave Mrs. Patterson a big sunhat and a bathing suit, imagining Moxie bottles in the sand.

"That stuff tastes awful," I said.

"We thought it tasted pretty darn good." He looked at his glass before putting it on the wooden table. "Whole lot better than this weasel piss."

"This stuff is terrible," I said, parking the glass on the porch floor. "Do you miss Mrs. Patterson?" I asked. It was a dumb question, but I wanted to hear him talk about her more.

He didn't answer directly. "My wife—no matter where we went—she wore red lipstick as bright as a stoplight. I always wanted to kiss her, but I knew I'd get that junk all over my face." He clasped his hands over his stomach. "Most of the time I did it anyway."

He must have read my mind because he said, "You think I always looked like this?"

I gave him the palms-up gesture. *Maybe.*

"When I look in the mirror, I think, 'Who *is* that old man?' I still feel like I'm nineteen years old. Honest."

I didn't know any nineteen-year-olds who sat on the porch all day and listened to a police scanner. But I liked the idea.

"I remember things from decades ago better than the stuff that happened last week. I remember when Stuffy Mc-Innis from Gloucester was traded to the Red Sox in 1917. Played with Babe Ruth in the 1918 World Series. Before the Curse. What a fielder!"

"Who's Stuffy McInnis?"

He threw his hands in the air. "Jesus, Mary, and Joseph. Lucy! He was part of the hundred-grand infield—Eddie Collins, Frank Baker, Jack Barry. But that was before his stint with the Sox."

"One hundred thousand dollars between four guys? He couldn't have been that good."

"These are 1909 prices!"

"Okay, okay. Tell me something else you remember," I said, even though I loved Sox trivia and riling up Mr. Patterson.

He scrunched his lips while he retrieved a thought. "My mother's rhubarb pie. She made it every June when my sisters and I were young."

"I like rhubarb pie," I said.

"I have a terrible sweet tooth."

"Do you like gummies?"

"Do I like what?"

"Gummies—Gummi Bears, Coke bottles, worms."

"No, I don't think so," he said, fanning himself with the *TV Week*. I forgot about the heat for a minute.

"You're pretty chatty today," I finally said.

"Maybe I'm delirious from the heat. It's a good thing you checked up on me." He grinned and gestured across the street to my driveway. "Your father doing okay today?"

"I don't know," I said. "He doesn't talk about himself much. Was he always like this?"

Mr. Patterson's brow wrinkled like he was thinking carefully about his answer.

"What do *you* remember?" he asked.

"I remember a real dividing line between what it was like before she died and what it was like after. They were just my parents and I didn't worry about anything."

Mr. Patterson nodded.

"But now, Dad seems a lot less happy. He works a lot. He used to read to me, or we'd draw together at night. We haven't done that in a long time."

"I knew your mom her whole life. She was born in that house, just like you were," Mr. Patterson said, pointing at my house again. "She was one of my favorite people on earth. And I remember when she started bringing your dad around. He was quiet even then, and we were all a little skeptical. But he turned out to be a good man. Took care of your grandmother when she got sick. And, boy, was he good with you when you were little. He'd take you on walks in the backpack all over town. He brought you and Fred down to the water and showed you the tide pools."

"So why is he so weird now?" I asked.

"I don't know for sure," Mr. Patterson said. "But I think it might be that your mother helped him connect with people. She invited his friends to dinner. She handed him the phone. If he was prone to turning inward, she helped him look outward. I know everyone is wired differently, Lucy, but you can't be an island."

I couldn't help looking at Mr. Patterson, sitting on his worn cushion beside the two radios, wondering if he was a bit of an island himself.

I took the photo of Mom, Dad, and Sookie out of my pocket and handed it to Mr. Patterson. He studied it closely.

"They were good friends." Mr. Patterson looked at me for a moment. "Tell your dad I'll be over to see if he needs anything at the store."

"I'll let him know," I said, peeling my legs off the porch planks. "I have to clean myself up."

When I walked in the door to my house, I headed straight to the bathroom for a shower. Dad was in the kitchen, eating a snack.

"Why do squids have three hearts?" I asked, walking up the stairs.

"Good question. I don't know," he said.

Before shedding my clothes, I took the photo out of my pocket and tacked it on my bulletin board. As I scrubbed off the fish guts, I thought about calling Vernon Devine, but I chickened out.

o o º o

I worked on some sketches for the field guide at the kitchen table. One of Mom's books was open to a photograph of a white shark. In my sketchbook, I drew the outline of the shark's body.

"I feel like all the sharks I draw look like sandbags," I yelled to Dad in the other room.

He half laughed. "What?"

Dad hobbled into the kitchen on one crutch.

"Like nothing is going on inside. Do they even have bones?" I said. "I get how the human body is put together, but I don't get what's happening inside a shark."

Dad started flipping pages until he came to an anatomy shot.

"*That's* what's going on," he said, pointing to an illustrated cross-section of a shark. I saw a number of labels for familiar organs—liver, kidney, intestines—but there was nothing human-like about the way the shark's organs were arranged. Besides, when I drew people I sometimes thought about muscles and bones, but never the heart.

"This isn't helping," I said.

"Here's the vertebrae. It's not bone. It's cartilage. It's lightweight and flexible, so they can move quickly," he said. "They don't have swim bladders, so heavy bones would make them sink."

I traced the backbone with my finger and decided to start with the shark's skeleton. I drew two pages of long, flexible zippers and noticed that a shark has no rib cage. I wondered what protected the organs or kept them in place.

o o º o

When Dad fell asleep on the couch again, I picked up the phone. I tried to picture what Vern would look like on the other end. Was he one of those old men with white hair like Jacques Cousteau who wore scuba suits well into their eighties? Who probably swam a mile in the ocean every morning before breakfast? Vernon Devine's phone rang six times before a woman answered.

"Hello?" she said.

"Uh, hi. I'm looking for Vernon Devine."

There was a pause, which gave me just enough time to realize what an idiotic idea this was.

"Vern is taking a nap now. Is there a message?"

"My name is Lucy Everhart. My mom was a shark

expert who worked with Vernon Devine. Her name was Helen Everhart. I found one of her research proposals from a few years ago, and I'm curious about an idea that she and Mr. Devine were working on when she died."

I took a breath and wished I hadn't said the part about her dying. Yes, it would probably make the woman on the phone feel sorry for me and I would have an easier time getting my message to Vernon, but sometimes I didn't like the pity I received when people found out I was motherless. It made me wonder if things were worse than I thought.

But the woman on the phone just kept an even voice and took down my information. "Okay, I think I have everything," she said.

There was another pause.

"Do you know about Vern, dear?"

"No, ma'am. I know nothing about Vern—other than the fact that he was my mother's mentor."

"He has dementia and talking on the phone has become difficult. When he picks up the receiver, he just stands there, quiet. He might listen to the things you say, but he won't say anything back."

"Okay," I said, feeling deflated.

"Where do you live?" she asked.

"Massachusetts."

"Would you be interested in coming to see him? If it's a good day, he can be quite talkative. It's really his short-term memory that is lacking, but he may remember your mom."

My mind was racing, but my lips were totally disconnected from my brain and I said, "Yes."

"Would you like me to ask him some questions about your mother? Maybe I can gauge whether or not the trip would be worthwhile."

"Yes, please."

"All right, Lucy. I will ask him when he wakes up."

"Are you Mr. Devine's wife?"

"Good Lord, no. I'm his nurse. My name is Marion."

"Nice to meet you," I said.

o   o   o   o

That evening, I took a break from drawing sharks to pick at a mysterious casserole with Dad. I was separating all of the mushrooms from the noodles when the phone rang.

"Hello?" I said.

"Hi, Lucy. This is Vern Devine's nurse, Marion."

"Hi," I said.

"I asked Vern about your mother this evening and I had to call you right away."

"Uh-huh," I said, anxious for the rest of the story.

"Vern led me over to some pictures on the wall and pointed to a photo of himself and a woman on a boat. And then he pointed to another photo of the same woman, and another. There were three pictures of this same woman on the walls of his library. I said, 'Who is that, Vern?' and he said,

'That's Helen.' I would say that he clearly remembers your mother."

"Okay," I said, not knowing what to say.

"Come and see Vern, Lucy. He would love to see you and I bet he'd be able to tell you something about your mom's project."

My heart was pounding. I looked at Dad with his mummified boot perched on a chair. There was no way he could ever drive with a broken right foot, even if he wanted to.

"I'll think about that. Thank you, ma'am," I said.

"What are you thinking about?" Dad asked when I hung up the phone.

"Nothing," I said.

But it was something.

21. Company Lunch

AT ALMOST NOON, I TOOK MY SECOND SHOWER SINCE FRED died. Under the steady stream, I was trying to figure out how to get to Maine to see Vern. I couldn't explain why I wanted to drive one hundred twenty-five miles to ask an old man with memory problems what he and my mom knew about the white sharks coming to Massachusetts. But I was certain that if Fred were here, he would be begging my dad to drive us.

When I turned off the water, I heard Dad calling my name.

"What?" I screamed back.

"Sookie and Lester are here," he yelled.

"What?" I yelled. "Why?"

"Lucy," he said, in tone that told me I was being rude. "Come down."

I stood dripping in the tub. If this was about cleaning fish, I wasn't going to be amused. It was hard to get excited about pulling fish bowels out of a good-looking mackerel and then repeating it a few hundred times, but more im- portant, I wanted to talk to Dad about going to see Vern.

When I rubbed the towel over my arms, my wrists looked

smaller, my freckled arms seemed gangly. I knew I hadn't been eating much because of the swallowing problem, but my body was starting to show signs of weight loss after only two weeks.

I raked a brush through my wet, gnarly hair and put the mermaid necklace over my head. I found some old clothes and headed down the steps, preparing to be marinated in fish entrails.

I followed the voices to the living room and saw Sookie and Lester with my dad.

"Hi," I said, hesitant to move farther than the doorway. The room felt smaller than usual, like the four of us were in a closet together. I stared at Lester. He'd lost a couple of pounds too, which Lester theoretically could have spared, but the new shape was wrong on him.

"You know I can't get on a boat," I said to Sookie.

"We're not takin' the boat out today," Sookie said. "We're going to lunch."

"Are you serious?" I asked.

"Yeah, why the heck not? Lucy, you're on the payroll. We're havin' a company lunch today. You wanna come?"

"Sure," I said. I was still having trouble swallowing food and I wasn't hungry, but I got the impression that company lunches didn't happen every day, and that I should accept.

"Well, let's get goin'."

o o °o o

A waitress named Susie put three plastic cups of soda on the counter and then pulled three straws out of her apron pouch without looking down. I scrunched the white paper down the straw, making a tight accordion. Then I picked up a drop of Coke with the bottom of my straw and sealed the top with my thumb. Using it like a dropper, I released a small splash of soda onto the crinkled paper, and watched it expand outward instantly.

"What's that?" Lester snorted.

I looked down at the wet mess on my paper placemat. "My mom showed me the trick when I was three. She called it 'the worm.'"

Lester nodded. He wasn't going to say anything bad about my mom.

"I could get used to this," Sookie said, taking a drag off his straw. He put his cup back on the counter. Sookie's hands were red and cracked like winter hands, and he had sausage fingers.

We talked about the Red Sox. I told Sookie and Lester the chatter I'd heard on Mr. Patterson's radio about the odds of the Sox calling up a shortstop from the minors named, Nomar Garciaparra.

"What's his name?" Lester asked.

"Nomar," I said.

Susie put a plate in front of me, and I looked at my burger

as if she had presented me with the side of a whole cow. It was going to be a challenge getting through it, no doubt.

"Watch your bait, Sookie," Susie said, as she delivered Sookie's meal. "Did you hear about that poor fisherman?"

"What? No," Sookie said.

"On the news, this morning," Susie said. "Guy was fishing with a rod. He reeled in his line and saw the fish had gotten away with half the bait. And then, wham! Shark comes up and snaps up the rest of the bait and swims away. Fisherman said it looked like a great white."

Sookie shook his head.

"Where did it happen?" I asked.

"Off the Cape," Susie said, shrugging. "You guys need anything else?"

I shook my head. I had plenty.

"Where are they all coming from?" Lester asked.

"I don't know," I said. "But they're looking for the seals."

"What time you want to go fishin' tomorrow?" Lester asked Sookie.

"Early. I got no excuse." Sookie manhandled his burger and ripped off about an eighth of a pound like a bear. "You busy tomorrow, Lucy?"

I tapped a fry on my plate, but before I could answer, Sookie asked, "Aren't you eatin' anything?"

I shook my head. "I can't swallow."

"Why not?" Sookie asked.

"I think it's nerves. From the accident."

I could feel Lester's body freeze.

"Thank you for searching for Fred." I covered his right hand with my left hand, which made him cry instantly.

"Good one, Lucy," Sookie said, passing Lester a wad of napkins.

"We shouldn't have taken you guys there in the first place," Lester said, wiping his nose on another napkin. "Let's talk about something else."

Sookie and Lester finished their burgers in silence, and Sookie ate a piece of apple pie. After Susie gave Sookie the check, I tested something random that had been on my mind.

"What kind of fish do harpoon fisherman go after?"

"Tuna. Swordfish."

I was glad Sookie didn't mention whales, but then he said, "Sharks."

I frowned.

"You used to use harpoons, right?" I said.

"I used to," said Sookie. "We use nets now, but we use a gaff all the time."

"A what?"

"It's a stick with a hook at the end," Sookie said.

"It helps you wrangle large fish," said Lester.

"Oh," I said. "But do you think you could still aim a *harpoon* and hit something?"

"Depends on what the something is," said Lester. "If it was a blue whale, Sookie could make contact."

"Funny," Sookie said in a flat voice. "Why did you ask? I didn't harpoon that shark, if that's what you're getting at. It got stuck in the net."

"I know," I said. "I just wanted to know if you were still capable of hitting one."

"Why?" he asked, looking at me with narrowed eyes.

"Just wondering."

○ ○ °○

Sookie paid the check, and he and Lester headed for the dock. I decided to stop at the mailbox to drop off another postcard for Fred. I walked by window boxes and tiny front yards crowded with bright flowers—tall zinnias, yellow daisy-like blooms, and pink roses had exploded like rashes on fences and arbors. Something about the sea was like steroids to the flowers through town. They grew strong.

I stopped in front of the bookstore and dropped the postcard into the mailbox. Mrs. Lynch, who worked at the bookstore, was standing in the doorway. She wore a long, flowy skirt with a Greenpeace T-shirt tucked into the waist.

"Hello, Lucy," she said, smiling.

"Hi, Mrs. Lynch," I said. When my mom was a kid, Mrs. Lynch had been her babysitter. It was hard to imagine Mrs. Lynch, with her gray hair, wrapped in a bun, as a teenager, dancing to music in the living room with my mom.

"You got a pen pal?" she said. "This is the second time I've seen you at the mailbox this week."

"Not exactly," I said. "Just sending postcards."

She looked at me with a serious expression, and it was as if she wanted to talk but couldn't find the words. I knew it was about Fred. I looked toward the water because I just couldn't handle another person looking at me like I was someone to feel sorry for.

"Lucy, Fred ordered a book," she said. "It came yesterday. It's paid for. Would you like to have it?"

"What is it?" I asked.

"Hang on a sec. I'll get it."

I followed her inside. I'd been in the bookstore a thousand times before. On hot days, Fred and I liked to take the spiral staircase downstairs and sit on the rug in the children's section, looking at books. I felt torn between wanting to bolt out the door and a vague curiosity about Fred's last book. While I waited for Mrs. Lynch to come back, I spun the postcard rack.

I pulled out one that was covered in different types of native saltwater fish and one that had an old Victorian drawing of a mermaid. I put four cards on the counter by the register and dug a couple of dollar bills out of my pocket. I almost left the money on the counter and disappeared, but Mrs. Lynch appeared with a thin textbook and placed it on the surface in front of me. It read, *The Biology of the Great White.*

I flipped through the pages. So many of my mom's books were general shark books, filled with pictures of all different types of sharks. Some had narrow, pointed snouts, like columns of new lipstick. Others had stubby heads with impressive, wide jaws. And then there were hammerheads, whose eyes branched off in far-reaching directions. But did they all look the same inside? Or were great whites built differently from others? I had wondered about this when I was drawing the backbone in my sketchbook.

"Thanks for the book," I said. She smiled. I knew it wasn't paid for in advance, that it was a gift from Mrs. Lynch.

I wanted to go down to the cool basement to read. I longed to hear Fred's sneakers on the metal steps behind me, but I wasn't ready to go down there alone. Right where I stood, I cracked open the shark book on a wide pile of new releases and started turning pages.

I looked at a table of measurements of white shark teeth with its tall columns of numbers for height, width, and angle. It was the sort of data that Fred would study until he found a pattern. I had almost dismissed the book when I turned the page and saw a photograph of a white shark's teeth, removed from the jaw and standing alone. Each white tooth was laid out on a black background in two straight lines, ordered from small to big. The tiniest tooth was like a pebble and tallest tooth was three centimeters high. But in between were a dozen teeth, each slightly bigger than the last, each a perfect enlargement of the one that came before it, like Russian dolls. The photo was a piece of art. I looked closer and noticed that the teeth weren't exactly the same. Some pointed straight and high like an equilateral triangle and others were angled like a sail in the wind. I zeroed in on the tiny, steak-knife ridges on the sides. These teeth were meant for tearing meat. My stomach growled.

At that very moment, I looked up and saw Fiona walk past the open door to the shop.

"I have to go," I said, closing the cover. "Thanks for the book."

"You're welcome," Mrs. Lynch said.

I gathered my postcards and stuffed them inside the pages. I headed out the door to see where Fiona was going.

22. Chinese Shoes

FIONA WAS ALONE. SHE WALKED TOWARD BEARSKIN NECK and I followed her, keeping a few paces behind. I wanted to talk to her, except I didn't really feel like talking to anyone. She wore olive pants and a white T-shirt that were both probably from the men's section of the Army-Navy Store. Her hair was wet, like she was just out of the shower. She carried a small black purse, the kind that was just big enough to hold a passport. I didn't own a purse.

After rounding the bend, she ducked into the Chinese import shop. I waited outside for a few minutes on the treeless road, wondering whether I should go in. I knew there was no hiding from Fiona in that tiny store. I took a breath and turned the doorknob.

A bell rang over my head and I closed the door behind me. The shop was crowded with racks of T-shirts, but there were also tiny satin pouches and silk pajamas with high collars. The reds and blues were as bright as oil paints.

Fiona was at the counter speaking with Mrs. Wong, the woman who owned the store.

"The red ones," said Fiona.

"Size eight?" asked Mrs. Wong.

"Yup."

"I'll help you next, Lucy," said Mrs. Wong, disappearing into the back of the store.

Fiona turned around and looked down the center aisle to where I was standing just inside the shop.

"Hi," she said, surprised to see me. Fiona was holding one of my favorite canvas shoes, the Chinese Mary Jane slippers. I'd probably owned a dozen pairs since I was a kid. My mom had bought them for me when I was little. At some point, I just starting asking Dad for money to buy new pairs.

"I love those shoes," I said.

"Me too," she said. Fiona looked a little tired.

o o º o

Fiona persuaded me to get an ice cream with her, and we walked to the end of Bearskin Neck with our cones. The coffee ice cream slid down easily and I started wondering whether I could survive on ice cream alone.

"How are you doing?" she asked.

"Okay," I said, looking at my hands.

When I didn't elaborate, she added, "What's that book?"

"Shark anatomy," I said.

"What are you doing with it?" she said, licking a drip from the bottom of her cone.

I told her about how I'd been working on the field guide (the one she had thrown out of Fred's window) and how

Fred and I had wanted to create a section for Sookie's shark. I explained that I wanted to get the drawings just right, but I thought it might help to understand the shark inside and out.

"Your projects are always so interesting," she said.

"Well, they were usually Fred's projects," I said.

She shrugged.

"But I'm kind of into it now," I said. "It's kind of overlapping with my mom's work. She predicted that the great whites would start heading north."

"Really?" said Fiona.

"Yeah, I found this research proposal she'd written before she died," I said. "It explains everything, but some of the details are a little over my head."

"You could bring it to Ms. Solomon."

"I guess so," I said, remembering Ms. Solomon outside the church at the funeral. Fiona looked a little distracted, like something was buzzing inside. "Are you okay?"

"I'm okay," she said. "Just worried about my mom, and Bridget's never around."

I nodded.

"How are you doing this?" she said, her brow wrinkling. "Your mom and then Fred. I can't even deal with Fred."

While I was thinking about what Fiona had said, I started choking on my ice cream cone.

"Are you okay?" Fiona asked.

"Yeah, it's normal. Since the accident anyway," I added. She looked puzzled.

"It's my brain," I said. "For some reason, I'm afraid I'll choke on my food. But then I make myself choke thinking about it. Remember the night in Fred's room when you threw his backpack out the window?"

"Yes."

"And I thought I was going to barf? That was whatever this is," I said.

She nodded and took a bite of her cone. "I used to be afraid of germs. Like, if the flu or a stomach bug was going around school, I would be freaking out."

"I don't remember that," I said, watching her swallow. "Not anymore?"

"A little, but it's much better."

"How'd it get better?"

"I'd try to imagine the worst thing that could happen, like getting the flu or barfing for a couple of days." She took another bite. "In the end, it just doesn't seem like that big of a deal. Unless you die from the flu, but that's rare."

"I don't know anyone who's died from the flu," I said.

"Me neither," she said.

We walked to the end of the peninsula and made a loop past the break wall and the wide ocean.

"I didn't figure it out on my own, though," she said. "I talked to Mr. Scanlon. Do you know him? The adjustment counselor at your school?"

I nodded. "He lives by Mill Pond."

She nodded.

I tossed the last of my cone in the garbage can and shifted the shark anatomy book, but the postcards fell onto the ground. Fiona popped the end of her cone into her mouth and wiped her hands. We both kneeled down to pick up the cards.

"These are cool," she said. "I love the mermaid."

"Take it," I said, handing the postcard to her. I wanted to ask her if she thought I was nuts for writing to Fred, but I didn't.

"Thanks," she said. She smiled as she took the card, but her face changed. She stared at my chest. I lifted my hand to the spot and felt Fred's gold necklace. It must have fallen out of my shirt when I picked up the cards.

"What's that?" she asked.

"It's a necklace," I said. "I found it in Fred's backpack."

It felt like a confession, as though I had stolen something that now belonged to Fred's family.

She reached out and I felt chills on the back of my neck as her nails slid over my cotton shirt. She gently pulled the pendant toward her for a closer look.

"It's beautiful," she said. "Another mermaid."

I nodded.

"Why did he have this?" she whispered.

"I don't know," I said.

"Do you think he wanted to give it to you?" she asked.

I shrugged.

"Did he ever say anything to you? I mean, about me?" I asked.

"All the time," she said. "But not like what you're asking. I used to annoy him about girls, but he never gave up any info."

She looked me in the eye and let go of the necklace. Then her brow wrinkled again. "What's it hanging from? Is that thread?"

"Dental floss," I said. "Cinnamon."

She shook her head. "You need something stronger than that."

"I know," I said.

We walked back down the Neck toward home.

"Who else would understand your mom's research paper?" Fiona asked. "Your dad?"

"Maybe." I didn't really feel like asking Dad about it. "My mom wrote it with a teacher of hers. I was kind of thinking of asking him about it. Only, I'd have to go to Maine to see him in person because he has dementia. It's a long story."

"You should go," she said.

"Seriously?" I said. "That's not weird?"

"No," she said. "I mean his memory isn't gonna get any better. What if he can tell you something about the project that no one else knows?"

I nodded. "But my dad can't drive 'cause of his foot."

"That's a problem," she said. "I'd take you myself, but I just went back to work last week. What about Sookie?"

I gave her a look.

"Seriously."

○ ₒ °○

At home, I opened the white shark anatomy book on the kitchen table. I slurped on a lime Popsicle, continuing my quest to survive on frozen treats, and leafed through the pages, wondering which part to draw next. I put the Popsicle in a glass and flipped through my sketchbook for a clean page, but halfway through, I paused at the moon snail drawings. I stopped breathing when I saw Fred's hand wrapped around the huge snail shell, his thin wrist and bulky watch. I remembered his fingers pulling the leaf out of my hair, making my head spin. He was alive then, just a few pages before now. I stared at the sketch until my vision started to double. I found the first blank page on the pad.

I made myself look at the anatomy book and I focused on the same picture for a while. I knew how the backbone worked, which really wasn't bones, and now I decided to try to make sense of the fins. A caption explained that fins were what made the shark an efficient swimmer.

I drew a dorsal fin on top and an anal fin on the bottom, to prevent the shark from rolling side to side when it was moving forward. I drew a pectoral fin on the side and a pelvic fin on the bottom to help the shark move up and down. I gave it a strong caudal fin—a tail—to allow the shark to swim side to side and propel it forward. The fins all had different jobs, like the wings of an airplane. While I still thought my mom was crazy for swimming with sharks, I wondered what it would look like to see those fins in action, to see a shark moving through the water.

Still, my great white looked like it was frozen on the page, a sandbag, accessorized by some deluxe fins. I wanted my drawing to look like it could swim to life with its torpedo body launching the shark at the speed of a car. I wondered which lines were the most important lines of the shark's shape—which ones made it a great white—and where did that powerful energy come from?

I pulled out the fish postcard. On it, I drew a pencil sketch of a shark, labeling the fins. Over the sketch, I wrote a note to Fred.

Native Saltwater Fish—Cape Ann, Massachusetts

Ran into Fiona in Mrs. Wong's shop . . . This is going to sound nuts, but are you sending me a great white every time I send you a postcard? (The kayaker chaser, the bait thief.) Just wondering.

1st dorsal fin

2nd dorsal fin

Pectoral fins

Pelvic fin

Anal fin

Caudal fin

POSTCARD

Fred Kelly

23. *Sookie Steps In*

THE NEXT MORNING, I WOKE UP FROM A DREAM, CRYING. I had been swimming up from deep, green water—the quarry—except it was light outside. The closer I'd gotten to the surface, the more I could see the sunshine. All I could think about was getting air and how good it was going to feel to break the surface, but when my head popped above the water, I realized that I had forgotten to bring Fred with me. When I looked down, he was nowhere in sight.

My pillow was sweaty. I felt terrified to be alone and I ran for the door, as though I'd seen a millipede skitter across the rug. On my way out, I stepped on a plastic animal figurine that had fallen off the top of my bureau days before. I grabbed the bottom of my foot and howled. Then I picked up the toy and hurled it into the far corner.

Before I made it to the living room, Dad called out, "Lucy, are you okay?"

He sat up on the couch where he'd slept and moved his leg with two hands, landing his boot on a pillow on the floor. All the time, he was looking at me, concerned.

"Are you limping?"

I nodded, crying louder.

He patted the cushion. I sat down close beside him, rubbed my foot, and told him about the dream.

"Look at me," Dad said.

I sucked in a large breath and looked at his wide, brown eyes.

"You couldn't have saved him," he said.

"No," I said. "But we shouldn't have been in the water."

"Lucy, it was an accident."

This didn't make me feel any better.

"It's not like it was when Mom died," I said.

"How so?" he said.

"I was little. I'm older now. And I know Fred is not coming back and I know exactly what that means."

Dad scratched the back of his head and said, "It's been five years since your mom died and sometimes I'm still waiting for her to come home. I have spent most of my time lately replaying the rescue in my mind, imagining how we could have gotten to Fred sooner." He shook his head and hesitated for a moment. "But it's out of my control now. I need to let it go, so the grief doesn't eat me alive."

"Which grief are you talking about? Mom or Fred?"

"Both."

"Yeah."

"I wish your mom were here now, so she could help us deal with Fred," Dad said.

My eyes burned. "I know."

There was a knock at the front door. I dragged the heel

of my palm over my nose, and I looked at Dad. He looked at me, as if to say, *You'd better get that because I'm not going anywhere for the next four weeks.* I rolled my eyes and went to the door.

There was Sookie, with two grocery bags from the IGA.

"I know it's early. I should have called," he said.

"No," I said. "Come in."

We went into the living room, where on the couch, the imprint of Dad's body was like a fossil, permanent and remarkably accurate.

"How you doin' today?" Sookie asked Dad.

"Fine," Dad said. "Just wish I could do more."

Sookie nodded. "Brought you some things for dinner tonight. I'll just put 'em in the kitchen."

I followed Sookie. He reached in and unloaded everything onto the counter. A rotisserie chicken, a couple of plastic tubs of things covered in mayonnaise, a watermelon wedge, a couple of bottles of Polar Seltzer, and a bakery bag of cookies.

"It's like a picnic," I said. "Thanks."

"No problem. I just want to help," he said. "You okay?"

My skin always turned red when I cried.

"Yeah, I woke up wrong," I said.

Sookie studied me hard and nodded.

In the living room, Dad had turned on the news. Sookie and I stood, watching a story about a house fire outside Boston. Footage of concerned neighbors looking at the blackened skeleton of a home transitioned abruptly to a grainy image of a dorsal fin sticking out of the water.

"Another potential great-white-shark sighting this summer," said the newscaster. "This time off the coast of Maine."

"What?" I said.

"It happens," Sookie said.

Apparently, a couple of Mainers were boating a few miles off Wells Beach and they spotted a large shark not far from the boat. Based on the witnesses' descriptions of size and the shape of the dorsal fin, area experts were trying to identify the type of shark.

On the TV, a shark expert explained the difference between the dorsal fins of the two huge sharks that were possible visitors to the area: great whites and basking sharks.

"That's Robin," Dad said. "Do you remember? She used to work with your mom."

I nodded. There was a bar across the bottom of the screen that read, DR. ROBIN WALKER, MARINE FISHERIES BIOLOGIST.

Robin had brown skin and black curly hair that was cut above her shoulders, which she pulled back with a wide headband. She was probably ten years younger than my parents and Sookie. She wore glasses and I wondered how she kept them on in the field.

"The dorsal fin on a basking shark is rounded on top and convex in the back," she said, making shapes with her hand. "White shark dorsal fins come to a point at the top and are straight on the back edge."

"Do you think it could have been a white shark?" the reporter asked her.

"It's possible," Robin said. "There's been an increase in recorded white sharks off the coast of Cape Cod. It's possible that some of them are traveling farther north."

The reporter said, "Why so many white sharks recently? Are you seeing a migration?"

"Good question," she said. "Historically, we've seen movement north in the summer and south in the winter. But I think the fact that we are seeing so many lately is largely due to the increasing seal populations."

"Do you have any advice for swimmers? For beach-goers?" asked the reporter.

"I understand the concern. If you see a seal, don't swim in that area," she said, emphasizing the word *don't* with her hands. "The possibility of being attacked is extremely low. So is getting struck by lightning. But when lightning strikes, don't run around your backyard and stand next to the flagpole."

Sookie snorted.

I nodded. I liked Robin.

"Well, I'm sure we'll have more information in the coming days," said the reporter. "Thank you, Ms. Walker."

"*Dr.* Walker," I corrected.

"Thank you," said Robin.

When the story cut out, I was buzzing with adrenaline. I followed Sookie out to his truck. Mr. Patterson was sitting on his porch across the street. It was already about a million degrees outside.

"What are you doing tomorrow?" I asked Sookie.

"Paintin' the boat," he said. "You wanna help?"

"No," I said. "I was wondering if you wanted to come up to Maine with Dad and me?"

"And do what?"

"Talk to an old guy about putting tags on great whites?" I said tentatively.

There was a pause. Sookie knew exactly what I was talking about.

"The trip might be a waste of time," I said. "Vern Devine's memory isn't so good. But the sharks are coming. Just like Robin said."

Sookie was still quiet. "Your dad wants me to come?"

"Yeah," I lied. I needed Sookie to come because I wanted him to hear about the tags, but more important, I needed him to drive. My dad was at least four weeks away from being allowed behind the wheel with that plaster boot.

"I might be able to find someone to help Lester paint the boat," he said.

We stood there for a bit. Mr. Patterson came down from his porch and walked across the street to the driveway.

"Hello, Sookie," said Mr. Patterson. "It's been a while."

"Hi," Sookie said, shaking hands with Mr. P.

"Don't let me interrupt," said the old man.

"No," said Sookie. "Lucy's just talkin' about takin' a trip."

"Where to?" asked Mr. P, looking at me with his eyebrows raised.

"Maine," I said.

He looked surprised. "Who's going?"

"My dad, Sookie, and me," I said, feeling guilty that I hadn't invited Mr. Patterson, even though the plans for the road trip had only started to solidify twenty seconds earlier.

"Sookie driving?" asked Mr. P.

"He'd kinda have to," I said, looking at Sookie, as if I were asking him formally. "On account of my dad's foot."

Mr. Patterson nodded again. "In the truck?"

I looked at Sookie.

Sookie frowned. "I think Lester would need the truck, so he could haul the boat to be painted."

I nodded.

"There's no AC in your dad's car," said Mr. Patterson.

This was true. It had gone out at the beginning of the summer and getting it repaired had slipped from the priority list to a slot far below "survival."

"Your dad's gonna need AC if he's gonna ride all the way with that boot," said Mr. Patterson. "Take my car."

Mr. Patterson pointed to the brown Dodge Diplomat, gleaming in the driveway as if it had been recently waxed. It probably had.

"It rides like a limousine," he said. "You know how to drive a limousine?"

Sookie smiled. "I think I could figure it out."

I wasn't sure just how Mr. Patterson's grampamobile translated to a limousine, but I felt so grateful that we might actually get to Maine that I blurted out, "You wanna come too?"

Mr. Patterson looked at me. Sookie looked at me.

"Why the heck not," said Mr. Patterson.

That just left telling Dad.

Later that night, in front of the Red Sox, I sat in the chair beside the sofa. Dad's leg was propped up, as usual.

"I am so tired of this couch," he said.

"I was hoping you'd say that," I said.

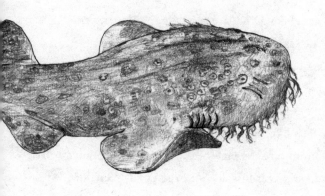

24. *Road Trip*

SOOKIE LICKED DORITO CHEESE FROM HIS FINGERS, AS THE Diplomat curved onto the bridge over the Piscataqua River. I threw off my seat belt, leaned between the headrests of the brown vinyl bench seat, and slapped my hand on the dashboard.

"Good Lord, Lucy. What are you doing?" Mr. Patterson asked from the seat beside me.

"I'm in Maine first!" I yelled, as we passed by the green sign on the side of the bridge that read, STATE LINE—MAINE.

I bounced onto my half of the back seat and quickly felt restless. I was so hungry that the pungent smell of Doritos made me want to hit someone. And the thing was, Sookie had offered me the chips twice, but I didn't have anything to drink and I knew I couldn't swallow them without a lot of liquid nearby.

As we coasted over the crest of the bridge, I looked out the window at the cargo ships and thought how odd it was to be headed out of state with Dad, Sookie, and Mr. Patterson. I had never been in a car with this particular combination of people. The thought was good material for a postcard to Fred, but I had used up my last card yesterday to tell him how I learned that white sharks have distinctly shaped dorsal fins and to thank him for sending that shark to Maine, so I could work up the guts to organize this weird road trip.

"I need to use the facilities," Mr. Patterson announced.

This seemed to nudge Sookie out of autopilot because he looked at Mr. Patterson twice in the rearview mirror. Maybe he was in disbelief that it was already time for a pit stop again.

Mr. Patterson pointed out the window. "Right there. Rest area."

Sookie looked over his shoulder and pulled off 95 North, toward the parking lot in a wooded area. Mr. Patterson opened his door and swung his legs over the threshold. He rocked back and forth in his seat, gripping the frame of the Diplomat, trying to propel his body out of the vehicle. *Isn't anyone going to help?* I wondered. Sookie rolled down the windows, turned off the engine, and just stared at Mr. Patterson. *Does he want anyone to help him?* I opened my door and went around to meet Mr. Patterson because it was the right thing to do, even if Mr. Patterson was going to yell at me for treating him like a child. Which was what he did. So I returned to my seat.

Mr. Patterson shuffled down the sidewalk to the little visitor's shack that probably smelled like a septic tank. Sookie pinched a coin and started rubbing a wad of scratch tickets he'd purchased at the gas station, and I stuck my face between the front seats.

"You doing okay, Dad?" I asked.

"Yeah," he said. "Luckily, it's not a long drive."

He had pushed his seat as far as it would go, so he could stretch out his legs. This left me with about as much legroom as a one-man submarine, but I didn't mind. I looked out the window and counted the number of people coming out of the visitor center. Within minutes, Sookie must have flaked enough scratch-ticket snow onto the floor mat to fill a coffee cup.

"Anything yet?" I asked. No answer.

"Anything yet?" I repeated.

"Forty bucks." He made a fart sound with his lips.

"That's good, right?"

"Not if I spent sixty."

"Why did you spend so much?"

"Something to do," he said, tossing the tickets on the floor. "You gotta win *sometime*."

"Lucy, you have to use the bathroom?" my dad said over his shoulder.

"Not *here*," I said. I never used public restrooms unless I was absolutely desperate. But I wondered if there were postcards in the visitor center.

Mr. Patterson came through the door and lowered his body back into the Diplomat. Sookie was checking the mirrors, ready to back out.

"Hold it!" I said. I grabbed my wallet out of my backpack and ran for the visitor's center. Next to the rack of maps and brochures, there was a collection of postcards that were so ugly the visitor center should have been giving them away. But they were five for a dollar, so I paid for a random assortment. On the way back to the car, I flipped through the stack, shaking my head.

"What did you get?" Dad asked.

"Postcards," I said.

"We're not staying that long, Lucy," he said.

I shrugged and cranked out a note to Fred in the back seat.

Photo of Loons on the Saco River.
Photo credit: Laurie Bowman.

Bad photography can ruin a couple of good loons.

POSTCARD

Fred Kelly

The pine trees along the side of 95 North grew dense and overwhelming past Kittery and Kennebunk. The majority looked like battered combs that were missing teeth. Thick, jagged greenery only covered the top quarter of the trees. It fit Maine. Rough, honest, make-do-with-what-you-got.

Past Portland and the first exits for Freeport, Dad helped

Sookie navigate a series of country roads overgrown with bushes and trees that blocked my view to the water. Finally, we spotted a mailbox that read 227.

"That's it," I said.

Sookie turned onto a long driveway that led to an old, white house. He stopped the car in front of a weathered barn and turned off the engine. We sat there, looking at the house, and I had a hard time remembering why we had come in the first place.

"What now, Lucy?" Sookie asked.

Through an arbor, I could see a deck off the back of the house with a view of a cove that belonged in a summer camp for rich kids.

"I have no idea," I said.

"Don't keep the man waiting," Sookie said, pulling the keys out of the ignition and opening his door in one motion.

I got out of the car and helped Dad out, holding his crutches as he pushed himself off the seat. He wore a plaid button-down shirt with chino shorts, and I thought about how long it had been since he'd worn clothes that could not be classified as either pajamas or underwear.

I stood on the gray slate stoop in front of him. The wooden screen door bounced open softly with each of his knocks, and a breeze churned the leaves on the big oaks surrounding Vern Devine's yard.

"Coming," said a voice inside the house.

She came into focus behind the wire weave of the screen.

We stepped back as the door swung outward. The woman had short gray hair and wore a pale pink blouse. Reading glasses hung around her neck on a brightly colored, woven cord, the kind from a global imports shop. I bet she knew how to meditate and made her own soap.

"Lucy?" she asked, looking at me.

"Yup," I said.

"I'm Marion."

"Thanks for inviting us," I said.

She smiled and introduced herself to my dad. Sookie and Mr. Patterson were making their way up the path.

"This is Sookie. He's a fisherman who my mom had asked to tag the sharks." I gestured to Sookie, who yawned before shaking Marion's hand. "And this is Mr. Patterson."

I left it at that because I had no idea why Mr. Patterson had joined us.

"Pleased to meet you," Mr. Patterson said, offering his hand to Marion.

"I'll take you inside. Vern is just waking up from a nap in his chair."

We walked into the house, following Marion. It was old, and the woodwork and creakiness reminded me of my house. I liked that Vern's walls were covered with artwork, mostly landscapes. We passed a telephone table, headed for the living room at the back of the house. There was a faint smell of urine that was erased by the breeze rolling through the window screens.

Outside the doorway, Marion stopped. She extended her arm, motioning us inside the room. In the corner, Vern sat in a reclining chair, covered in a large, baby-blue blanket. He was a small man with a round face and giant glasses. His big eyes, magnified, blinked and stared at us, searching, though he smiled peacefully.

"Vern," Marion said. "Helen's daughter, Lucy, is here. You remember Helen, your student. The shark lady."

"Of course. Come in," he gurgled, clearing his throat.

I figured I was delusional in thinking I might make sense of my mother's last research project by coming to this house. Vernon Devine seemed more frail than I had imagined. I moved closer to the recliner.

"Professor Devine, this is my dad, Tom, and my friends, Sookie and Mr. Patterson." The men all shook hands.

"It is good to see you again, Vern," said Dad. "I'm Helen's husband, Tom."

"Yes, of course," he said, though I got the sense that Vern did not recognize my dad. He looked down at Dad's cast. "You look like you're in a bad way."

We were all quiet until Mr. Patterson said, "Tom is a rescue diver. He broke his foot in a very difficult rescue effort."

Vern looked at the boot again and then he scanned our faces.

Marion went over to a comfortable-looking chair in the room and motioned for my dad to come sit down.

"It's a recliner," she said. "Come put that foot up."

Dad settled into the soft chair and she popped the footrest.

Vern blinked, flashing his enormous brown eyes. "Where are you from?"

"Rockport," I said.

"Rockport?" he asked. "*I* was born in Rockport. Come sit down."

I was confused, but then realized that maybe *he* was confused.

He pointed to the couch and to another chair by the coffee table. Mr. Patterson took the chair, while Sookie and I sat on the couch. Marion stood.

"My oldest brother was born in 1891. The year Rockport split from Camden."

Where the heck is Camden?

"You mean Rockport, *Maine*," Sookie said.

"Sure," said Vern Devine.

"We're from Rockport, Massachusetts," Sookie added.

"Really? Would you like a soda?" Vern asked, looking around at his guests.

"We have ginger ale and Moxie," Marion chimed in.

"Moxie, please!" Mr. Patterson exclaimed. It was the most animated he'd been all day.

Marion set the sodas on the coffee table and handed one of the orange cans to Mr. Patterson. He popped the top and drank the bitter beverage, swallowing with his eyes closed. "Mmm. That is first-rate."

Sookie and I cracked open the cans of Canada Dry.

"Why did Rockport split from Camden?" Dad asked.

Vern took a slurp of the Moxie and said, "I don't remember exactly. Some days I'm as sharp as a tack and others, I can't remember my own son's name. My father was a quarryman."

"Ha!" Mr. Patterson snorted. "*My* father was a quarryman."

"Limestone?" asked Vern.

"No. Granite," said Mr. Patterson.

Here we go, I thought. Men from Rockports, talking rocks.

Mr. Patterson and Vern Devine continued on for twenty-five minutes. Vern told us how limestone from Rockport, Maine, was sent to Washington, DC, to build an important building, which he later remembered to be the Capitol building. Mr. Patterson explained how his father and three hundred other quarrymen went on strike days before the stock market crash in 1929, never to return to work in the pits again. They talked about the navy and their wives. And then Vern said, "I don't know who you people are, but I'm having a great visit."

Marion came back into the room to give Vern some pills in a white cup. His hands shook like a bobble-head doll when he reached for the medication.

"Sookie is a fisherman," I told Vern, pointing at Sookie. "About a month ago, a great white shark swam into his net by accident. An eighteen-footer."

"Is that so?" Vern asked, focusing on Sookie. "Where were you fishing?"

"About twenty miles off Rockport." He added, "Massachusetts."

"Wait a minute," said Marion. "That made the papers up here."

She disappeared into the hall.

"Can I try a sip of that?" Sookie asked Mr. Patterson.

"My Moxie?" Mr. Patterson's eyes widened.

"Yeah. I'm curious. I don't want to take a whole can."

Sookie reached for Mr. Patterson's drink, took a sip, and made a face like he had ingested a mouthful of motor oil. "That is sickening."

"It's an acquired taste," Mr. Patterson said, taking back his can.

"We like it," said Vern.

Marion returned with the clipping.

"I cut this out for you," she said, showing the article to Vern. She looked at Sookie. "That's you?"

"Yes, ma'am." Sookie's fifteen minutes of fame had been extended by two seconds. He blushed.

"I remember. That was a big one," Vern said, pointing to the photograph. "Sad, really."

"Vern, let's show them the photos of Helen in your study," said Marion, changing the subject. She helped Vern to his feet without giving him the option of declining.

We followed Marion and Vern back into the hallway and

into a room off the back of the house with views of the Casco Bay cove. Vern's study was lined with bookshelves and a collage of framed photographs. There was a black-and-white picture of Vern leaning over a giant octopus sprawled out on a lab table. Vern looked younger, except he wore the same bug-eyed glasses. There was a photo of four children in bathing suits, with their legs dangling from a dock.

"Who are they?" I asked.

"Those are my children," he said. "They're retired now. Can you believe that?"

I smiled.

Just above my head, my eyes drew like magnets to another photograph: my mom and Vern. I gasped.

It was so odd to see her here in this old man's house. I knew she had a life outside of us, but here was the evidence. They both wore diving masks around their necks and blue sweatshirts. If Vern was ninety-five years old, he must have been scuba diving and teaching into his eighties. He must have liked his job.

"How old was my mom in the picture?" I asked Vern.

Vern looked at Marion. Marion looked at Dad.

Dad leaned on his crutches and studied the photo. "She was probably in her early twenties."

"Gosh, you look like her," Marion said.

We both had a slew of freckles, but her hair was more brown than red, and she didn't have zits. I thought of the conversation I'd had with Fiona at Newbury Comics. I hoped I ended up looking like my mom.

"There's one over here." Vern pointed his shaky hand to another image of my mom. This time, she was in a group of people, standing at the water's edge, looking at a dorsal fin poking out from the flat calm. "That was a bull shark. It was trapped in a salt pond on the Cape."

Under the surface, the shark looked huge, not that different from a white shark.

"How'd you get it out?" I asked Vern.

"We didn't do anything, except watch. For days. The full moon came and raised the tide. The deeper water helped the shark swim back into the ocean."

I looked at Vern, wondering how he could remember details like that, yet not know how to use a telephone anymore. He blinked his big eyes.

There was another photo of my mom and Vern at the front of a classroom. He was leaning against an island with a sink at the front of the room and she was talking to the students.

"I was still teaching at the university," Vern said. "And Helen must have been a guest lecturer in my class that day."

My mom was smiling and doing something weird with her hands and the college kids were awake, at least the ones I could see in the photo. Dad leaned into the photo and studied it closely.

"Every once in a while, you get a student who knows

her stuff. And that was your mom," Vern said. "She knew her stuff better than anyone else I ever taught."

I smiled at Vern and he smiled back.

"Vern, you doing all right?" Marion asked. "Want to sit down?"

"Yes," he said.

Marion helped him into a chair.

"I'm going to make a few sandwiches. You are welcome to visit with Vern in the study as long as you'd like," said Marion. "He does get tired, so don't be surprised if he nods off on you. And call me if he starts getting feisty."

"Don't take it personally," said Vern, clasping his hands on his lap.

I thought I should run out to the car and grab the research proposal before Vern fell asleep, so I left the men in the study and returned with my backpack. Sookie and Vern were talking about the depleting cod population in the ocean. I waited for a lull.

"Professor Devine, I wanted to show you the research proposal you wrote with my mom about tagging great whites. I'm trying to understand the details."

I set the paper in Vern's lap and he slowly began to flip through the material, stopping after only a few pages.

"Yes. This was Helen's baby. I contributed very little, but she had a great idea."

"What made it great?" I asked.

Dad shifted his weight, scuffing his boot on the wood floor.

"Do you know what the 'census' is?" Vern asked.

"Kinda?"

Vern opened his mouth to speak, but then looked puzzled. "Can somebody explain the census?"

Mr. Patterson spoke up. "Every ten years the United States government collects data to find out who is living in the US. The census takers ask questions about age, sex, and race, to see how the country is changing."

"It's friggin' annoying. If you don't send in your form fast enough, they start callin' your house," Sookie said. "No thanks. I'd rather stay off the grid."

Dad smiled.

Vern ignored Sookie. "There is no census for white sharks. We have no idea how many young sharks, middle-aged sharks, and old sharks there are. A balance would tell us there is a healthy . . ."

Vern was searching for the word.

"Ecosystem?" Dad offered.

"Correct. If there is an imbalance . . ." Vern hesitated. "There might be a problem."

Vern was slowing down. I had been standing up the whole time we were in the study and I crouched to a squat, hanging on to the arm of Vern's upholstered chair. Vern took off his glasses and rubbed his eyes. When he put the glasses back on, he looked straight into my eyes and put his hand on top of mine.

"You'll get your census data, Helen," he whispered.

My neck and shoulders were tingling. I wanted to correct him, but I just stared at his mouth, wondering what he would say next.

"You'll figure out what those sharks are doing here."

He blinked and smiled at me. I was almost a thirteen-year-old, but he thought I was a shark expert. Whatever fog his mind might have had, there was a clear line that led straight back to Mom. I didn't know what else to do, so I went for it.

"Okay," I said. "How do I find the sharks, if nobody knows where they are headed?"

"In a plane," he said.

"Should I get the nurse?" Sookie whispered.

I kept looking at Vern. "You think I should get on a plane?"

Vern shook his head. "No. It's like we talked about. A man is in the plane . . . he will call you on the boat."

It sounded like nonsense to me, until Dad said with the sureness of a dart, "A spotter."

I turned to face my dad. "A what?"

"I'll explain later," he said. His brow was creased.

"But, Helen, wait for the seals," Vern said.

Vern took a deep breath and closed his eyes. He was asleep.

I stayed in a squat, watching Vern breathe for a moment, and then I fell onto my butt, looking around at everyone.

"If I ever get like that, just take me out to pasture and shoot me," Sookie said softly. I looked up at Vern to make sure he was still asleep.

Dad was rubbing his chin. "Hold on. Some of the things he said make sense. Spotter planes are used to find fish. Lucy, hand me the proposal."

The pages were spread across Vern's lap. I pinched a corner, pulled the paper away from the professor's knees, and passed it up to my dad. Vern didn't flinch.

"Do you remember the spotter plane?" he asked me.

"No." I had taken a break after the part about the harpoon boat.

"I remember it," said Sookie. "The spotter plane was going to keep an eye out for the sharks and radio to the boat to help the captain get the right position."

He looked over Dad's shoulder at the proposal.

"Christ, Helen. Might as well hire Roger Clemens to fly the friggin' plane." Sookie gave a budget presentation on his fingers. "First, you gotta pay the fisherman for his fuel and his time. Then, you gotta pay the spotter to find the shark." He shook his head. "The state's not gonna pay for that."

"She was looking for grant money," Dad said.

"What did he say about seals?" asked Mr. Patterson.

Dad looked like he was about to answer when Marion walked into the room.

"You bored him to death," she said, covering Vern's lap with a colorful afghan.

Vern's head was tipped to the right, and he breathed through his mouth.

"Actually, I think we wore him out," Mr. Patterson said.

"That's possible," said Marion, picking up a water glass from the table beside Vern's chair. "Lunch is ready."

Marion led us to the round wooden table in the kitchen. The lazy Susan in the center held a strange combination of items—a number of prescription drugs, a set of binoculars on top of a bird guide, and an animal bone.

As we chose our places, I asked, "What's the bone?"

Marion put a platter of sandwiches and a glass bowl of tortilla chips onto the table. "I found that down by the rocks this morning. I was going to ask Vern where it came from. It keeps him sharp."

Fred would have already generated a short list of potential candidates. I looked at the bone. Maybe a rabbit, or a cat, or a groundhog. Something small, but not chipmunk small. I thought about how I would draw it on the back of a postcard to Fred.

"Thank you for making us lunch," Dad said. "You didn't have to do that."

"Of course. I was happy that you could make the trip. I think Vern is happy too."

"How long have you been Vern's nurse?" I asked, taking a sandwich from the platter and passing the dish to Sookie. I pulled the bun off my sandwich and started ripping it into bite-size pieces.

"Well, Vern originally hired me to take care of his wife, Eleanor, when she was battling cancer. When Eleanor passed away two years ago, Vern started showing signs of dementia, so I just stayed on to help him. It seemed meant to be."

"He seemed pretty with it today," said Sookie. "I mean, when he was remembering the shark that got stuck in the pond."

"His long-term memory is still impressive. It's the short-term memory that is failing him. And he gets crabby sometimes. But all in all, he's still doing pretty good."

Dad poured me a drink and I put one of the bread pieces in my mouth, chasing it with a sip of lemonade. It went down smoothly, but after a while I lost interest in eating because it took so long to choke down the food.

"Were you able to get the information you needed from Vern?" Marion asked.

"Well," I said. "Sort of. We did get some new information, but it just made me want to ask more questions and then Vern fell asleep."

Marion nodded. "You just write down your questions after lunch and I'll see what I can find out."

o o º o

Dad, Sookie, and Mr. P ate cookies and decided to take a walk out back to get a better look at the cove. I stayed behind in the kitchen and looked out the picture window with the binoculars, spotting a small boat moored close to Vern's property.

"Is that Vern's boat?" I asked.

"Yes. His son usually takes him out a couple of times during the summer for a short ride."

"You get a lot of birds around here?" I asked.

"We do," Marion said, setting a glass in the drying rack. "Want to bring me your plate, Lucy?"

"Sure," I said.

She scraped my dish into the trash and dropped it into the soapy water. "You didn't eat much. You don't like cold cuts?"

"Cold cuts are fine," I said.

"It's none of my business, but have you always been very thin?" she asked.

I put down the binoculars and felt my stomach flip, as though I'd been cornered. "Well, sort of, but I have been having problems swallowing this summer. It makes me not want to eat."

She brought a glass of lemonade to the table and sat down.

"Any idea why?" Marion asked.

"Yeah," I said.

I told her about the accident and losing Fred. I told her about how I sometimes feel like I'm going to die at mealtimes or choke on my own saliva.

"Have you seen a doctor about the swallowing?"

"Not exactly. Dad talked to a nurse on the phone. She said it might be anxiety."

"She's probably right. Two huge losses," she said. "Panic attacks seem like a normal response to me."

I shrugged. "Great."

"Here's what you do," Marion said. "Start with soft foods—applesauce, Jell-O, soup. Make it easy on yourself at first."

I nodded.

"Then you need to say to yourself a few times, 'My body knows how to do this.' And you let your body do its job."

"That sounds too easy." I poked the animal bone with my finger. Maybe it came from a fox.

"It is, if you stop getting in the way." Her expression was neutral.

"Okay," I said, picking up the binoculars and looking out the window again. I saw Mr. Patterson plucking berries off a bush. The binoculars felt like a mask that put some distance between Marion and me. "When I was talking to Vern, he got confused and thought I was my mom. Does that happen a lot?"

"Sometimes," said Marion.

"He called me *Helen* and told me it's my job to collect data on sharks."

"Maybe it is."

"But he meant that *Mom* is tracking the sharks."

"Some days it's hard to know when Vern is talking crazy and when he's making sense."

25. The Presence
of a Lady

WE WAITED FOR ABOUT AN HOUR AFTER LUNCH, BUT VERN was officially worn-out. There was no chance of getting any more information about Mom's research or the tagging project. I wrote down a few questions for Marion, not knowing if we'd still be in Maine to visit the next morning.

At a gas station, Sookie sat behind the wheel while he waited for the pump to click off. A map was spread over Mr. Patterson's lap.

"Let's stay at a motel," Mr. P said. "My treat."

I poked my head between the front seats.

"Uh," Dad said, looking into the side mirror, probably hoping for an out. "Sookie, do you need to get back tonight?"

Sookie was leaning on the armrest with his forehead in his palm, dozing. "Nah, Lester's painting the boat all week."

It was quiet for a moment. "Why do you want to stay?" Sookie asked Mr. Patterson.

"I just like being here. That's all," he said. His knee was bouncing around like his feet were doing a little dance.

I looked at the islands scattered along the lower half of Mr. Patterson's map and settled into the back seat to dig up a postcard for Fred.

o o °o

After some debate, we pulled into the Spruce Grouse Lodge. It seemed a little rustic, with cars pulled up to the guest room doors and rooms only on the ground level. I dropped my backpack in a room with my dad that smelled like furniture polish and lemon candies and decided to hike down the sidewalk for a side-by-side comparison of the accommodations. Sookie was sitting on the bumper of the Diplomat, drinking coffee. Fred would've disapproved of the Styrofoam cup.

I knocked on Sookie and Mr. Patterson's door.

"It's open," Mr. Patterson said.

The room was identical to ours, but I lingered to watch the old man unpack. He was the only one in our group who thought to bring an overnight bag. Mr. Patterson arranged his toiletry kit, clothes for tomorrow, and pajamas on the bed. Everything looked ironed. He sifted through a plastic bag of pill bottles, lining up cylinders on the bedside. This was my neighbor, who had sat on his porch in his undershirt for most of my life. I imagined him wearing the same pajamas for weeks, if he even cared to wear them at all. Yet he was as deliberate about setting up his motel room as a military ritual.

"I wish I'd brought the scanner," he said, placing a pair of slippers on the bedspread.

"What kind of reception would you get? We're in a freaking pine forest."

"Lucy, watch your mouth." Then he got quiet. "You are in the presence of a lady," he said, lifting a wooden box out of the suitcase. He held it flat in his palms. It looked like a fancy cover for a tissue box.

"What's that?" I asked, pointing.

We locked eyes and he said, "Mrs. Patterson."

"What?"

"It's an urn."

"Like for *ashes*?"

"Yep."

"Why didn't you bury her in a coffin?"

"She didn't want to take up so much space."

"What is she doing *here*?" I was clearly not the only one with a plan.

He sat down on the foot of the bed with the box on his lap. "After the funeral home gave me the urn, I walked it up to the Headlands. I climbed out on the rocks and tossed half of her into the sea. Then I got cold feet. Maybe I didn't want to get rid of the whole thing just yet. I brought the rest home and put her on my dresser."

"Now what?" I asked.

"Tomorrow morning we could get a boat. Go out to French's Island," he said in a calm voice, as though it were as simple as going to lunch. But then he looked me in the eye and his brow wrinkled. "You think your dad would go for it?"

Would he go for it? No. But French's Island was the spot in Maine where Mr. Patterson used to drink Moxie and sit on the beach with his wife when they were young. He probably wasn't going to make it to Maine ever again.

"I'll talk to Dad," I said.

Sookie walked back into the room. "I'm goin' to the front desk to get a cup of coffee. Anybody want anything?"

"I'll come," I said.

My eyes wandered around the motel lobby. There were odd things for sale in baskets on the counter. Sailors' rope bracelets—the kind that shrink to the wrist. Embroidered sachet pillows that smelled like pine, probably handmade. And key ring flashlights. Beside the cash register was a spinning kiosk of postcards—ten for $1.00. A bargain. I realized I was already the owner of nine blank postcards featuring photos of loons and lighthouses, but I had the urge to hoard.

"Hey, Sookie, can I borrow a buck?"

He pulled a single out of his billfold.

The choices were moose, loons, and lobster. I took three of each and grabbed an extra moose. Back in the room, I wrote a note to Fred and I stuffed the rest in the field guide.

Moose in the moonlight, Casco Bay.
Photo credit: John Ross Tinkerman

We met Vern Devine today. I think I arrived about three years too late to get a clear interpretation of the research proposal, but he gave some clues – a spotter plane and seals. Vern thought I was Mom and it was kind of like talking to Yoda, or something. He called me the "Census Taker." (What?!) Dad said he would explain it all at dinner. By the way, I'm in a crappy motel with Dad, Sookie, and Mr. P. It's awesome.

POSTCARD

Fred Kelly

_____

_____

I thought about giving the note to the man at the front desk to mail, but when I tried to explain the missing stamp and address in my head, I sounded like a lunatic. So I tucked the postcard into my back pocket, in case we saw a mailbox.

Later that night, Dad and I burrowed into our matching twin beds.

"How's your foot?" I asked.

"It's all right," he said. "I wish I had Vern Devine's recliner."

"Hey, Dad?" I asked.

"Yeah."

"Can we rent a boat?"

"Here?" he said. "Or at home?"

"Here."

"I don't think I'm up for boating yet," he said. "And we need to get home."

"You can stay on land," I said. "Sookie can drive."

"Why do you want a boat?" he asked. It was a good question, seeing that being near water was traumatic.

"I need to do a favor for Mr. Patterson," I said. "He needs to scatter Mrs. Patterson's ashes on French's Island."

"Wait, what?" Dad said. I heard him roll over in the dark.

"She's been sitting on his dresser for years. He said it's time," I said. "I think we should help."

"He brought her *ashes*?"

"I know. It's weird. But, Dad, he never asks us for anything."

He sighed. "*Luuuucy*. Where the heck is French's Island?"

"Somewhere in Casco Bay."

"It's a big bay!" he said, raising his voice.

"Why don't we look at a map and then we can decide?" I said.

"Where are we going to get a boat?" he asked.

"We'll figure it out."

26. *Interconnected*

IN THE MORNING, I REMEMBERED THAT VERN DEVINE HAD A boat, but Sookie remembered it was a sixteen-foot Boston Whaler Eastport with a four-stroke seventy-horsepower outboard. Marion told us we could take it out, so long as we paid attention to the tides.

Sookie and Dad read the charts and determined that French Island, or "French's Island" as Mr. Patterson called it, was a reasonable ride for a small boat. In fact, it was eerie how close it was to Lower Flying Point, where Vern lived.

We went out for breakfast, where I ate a bowl of oatmeal with a heap of brown sugar that melted into syrup over the hot mush. In small spoonfuls, it went down smooth with a glass of milk and it made me feel full, which had become a foreign concept. We stopped at a gas station on the way and picked up a six-pack of Moxie at Mr. Patterson's request. And on the way back to Vern Devine's house, I spotted a mailbox, so I dropped my postcard to Fred inside.

Near high tide, we walked down the wooden staircase to the rocky shoreline. I wasn't crazy about cruising around the bay, and setting foot in the boat made me regret the idea of heading out to the island. But when I looked at Mr.

Patterson, who was trying to get a good foothold in the rocks with the urn tucked under his arm, I just kept walking down the stairs one foot in front of the next. We waved to Marion and Dad as they watched us from the deck.

Mr. Patterson read a chart of Casco Bay, and Sookie steered us closer to a scatter of islands covered in tall pine trees. My chest was tight underneath the life vest, like the way it had felt at mealtimes lately when I was staring down a plate of food. I thought about what Vern's boat looked like from below, imagining the growing distance between the floor of the bay and the boat's hull. The water was dark and, in my mind, as bottomless as the quarry.

I imagined a long, dark shadow passing by our little boat.

"What's wrong?" Mr. Patterson said to me. "You look nervous."

"I'm fine," I said, but I was wishing I hadn't dropped that postcard in the mailbox. What if Fred sent me another one of his white sharks while we were floating in this bathtub-size boat?

"Can great whites come into Casco Bay?" I asked, hoping the sharks avoided swimming in bays.

"They could," Sookie said.

We rose and fell over the swells of a larger boat, but I kept my eyes on the trees. Mr. Patterson, dressed in pressed pants and a button-down shirt, held the urn tightly to his life jacket while we pushed on into the bay.

After the swells died down, I pulled my hands into the sleeves of Marion's sweatshirt and looked around. I thought I saw a yellow lab in the waters ahead.

"Is that a dog?" I asked.

"Seal," yelled Sookie.

Two of them bobbed in the water, not far from the Whaler. Seals were all over Cape Cod, but I had never seen one in Rockport.

"Holy fish," I said, eyeing the seals with their sleek heads and black noses. I looked for dorsal fins in the water, as Mr. Patterson directed Sookie around the islands.

o o º o

On the beach of French Island, Mr. Patterson took the urn in two hands and shook it up a little. He flung Mrs. Patterson in an arc at the water's edge. The white-gray cloud settled into the Atlantic, becoming part of the silt and rocks below. Sookie cracked open a Moxie and we sat on a slab of rock while Mr. Patterson looked over the sea. Sookie offered me a can and I accepted.

"I'm getting used to this junk," said Sookie, resting the orange can on his knee.

"Not me." I shivered.

"Why did we bring it out here?" Sookie asked, taking a sip.

"In honor of Mrs. Patterson," I said. "She and Mr. P

used to bring it with them when they had picnics out here."

Mr. Patterson looked over his shoulder to see what we were up to.

"Should we go check on him?" I asked.

Sookie said, "He probably wants to be alone."

"Nah. I'll go see if he's okay," I said.

When I stood beside Mr. Patterson, I saw his wet cheeks. The toes of his loafers pointed so close to the tide, they turned dark brown. I took his hand.

o o º o

When we returned to the cove, Vern was sitting on the deck with a blanket over his lap. Marion was reading a magazine on a chaise lounge.

"Vern, could I ask you a question?" I said.

"Of course, dear."

"What happens if great whites become extinct?"

Marion looked up from her magazine.

"All life is interconnected. If one species moves away or becomes extinct, the order shifts," said Vern. "What happens in the ocean, affects the life on land. It's Darwin's theory."

There was a pause again and then Vern said quietly, "Remind me who you are."

"I'm Lucy, Helen's daughter," I said.

"You're looking after the sharks," he said.

"That's right," I replied.

"Sharks have few offspring, which makes it easy for them to become extinct. But maybe we can still reverse what we've done to them."

"How?" I asked.

"Stop eating them. Learn about their behavior. Respect that they have been here far longer than any of our human relatives," he said.

I nodded, though I had no idea what to do with this information.

"Would you like to go for a ride on the boat?" Sookie asked Vern and Marion as he walked up the steps to the deck.

Marion lowered her magazine and looked at Vern. "What do you think, Vern? You up for a boat ride today?"

"I could do a short ride. Yes, that would be nice," said Vern, squinting in the light, as he looked up at Sookie and took his offered hand.

Vern and Marion took their life jackets from Mr. Patterson and me and piled into the boat with Sookie. I watched them cruise in and around the cove in the Whaler, with Vern wrapped in a blanket as if he had already fallen in.

Mr. Patterson sat on the deck beside me.

"If I drink any more Moxie, I think I'm going to develop an ulcer."

"I told you that stuff was no good," I said.

"I didn't say it wasn't good."

"That's a double negative," I said. "I'm gonna go inside."

I had been wanting to look at the photos of Mom again. I opened the slider and walked into the kitchen. The wood floors creaked as I moved to the study, where I found Dad, leaning on his crutches, looking at the photos on the wall.

"Hi," he said.

I walked over to the spot where he was standing.

"Which one were you looking at?" I asked.

He pointed to the one where Mom was speaking to the students in Vern's class.

"I took that photo," he said.

"Really?" I looked closer.

Mom had her hair in a ponytail, her mouth was open like she was talking, and she was making a weird two-handed gesture, like she was cradling an imaginary volleyball. I'd seen that geeky excitement before from a few of my teachers at school. She was aiming that volleyball at one of Vern's students and she was either congratulating him on his brilliance, or coaxing him to push one of his ideas to the next level. The funny thing was, she didn't look much older than the kids in the class.

With his camera, Dad had caught her being real. She was frozen in that strange position, with her mouth open, in the middle of a word, but it was a piece of truth. I wondered what the word was.

"When did she become interested in science?" I asked.

"Maybe junior high? High school?" he said.

"Was she like Fred? I mean, did she always keep aquariums and hang out in gross places?"

He squinted. "Not when she was really young, like Fred did. We had a good science teacher in junior high. That might have been the turning point."

I nodded.

"Weird to see her picture in somebody else's house. *Your* picture," I said.

"Definitely," he said, moving his eyes to another photo. "But good, right?"

"Yeah," I said. "He thinks she was special."

Dad looked at me and smiled. "Exactly."

That was the crazy thing. Vern was losing his mind, but he still remembered my mom. She was *that* good.

"Did you take a lot of pictures of her?" I asked Dad.

"Tons," he said.

"Where are they?"

"On the walls. In the closet. Look around the house," he said.

While I felt proud that my mother was brave enough to swim with sharks, teach sharkology to college kids, and track shark movement and behavior to fill books and classrooms with new information, I also felt frustrated. What happened to the idea of tagging the sharks? Did her work just stop after she died? Or did it keep moving ahead?

When Marion, Sookie, and Vern returned, Vern hung on to Marion's arm and moved slowly, but his eyes were wild like he'd just come off the Zipper at the Topsfield Fair.

"I love the smell of mud," he said.

I smiled. The bay reeked like farts, but okay.

"Hey, Vern, can I ask you something?" I said.

"Of course, dear."

I wondered if he knew I was me, or if he thought I was Mom. "Has anyone tagged the sharks yet?"

"I should think not. Not without you."

I looked at Vern's wide eyes behind his big glasses.

"What did you mean when you said, 'Wait for the seals'?"

Vern extended his hand from under the blanket and touched my arm. "They're coming back. That island is going to be full of them," he said, spitting on my shirt. I didn't mind.

"Which island?" I asked.

"The one in your paper."

I nodded.

"Keep collecting your data," he said, patting my arm.

o o º o

It was getting dark outside by the time we got on the highway to head back home. Dad and Sookie were up front again and Mr. Patterson and I were in the back seat. I pulled out a postcard of a moose against an autumn leaf backdrop and used the field guide as a table.

"You need better light than that," Mr. Patterson said. He tapped my dad's shoulder and said, "Tom, there's a flashlight in the glovebox. Would you mind?"

Dad fished around in the glove compartment and passed a small light behind his headrest.

"Thanks," I said.

Bull Moose, Baxter State Park, Millinocket, Maine
Photo credit: Jon Schultz

We took Mrs. Patterson's ashes out to an island in Maine and Mr. P emptied the urn into the bay. Kind of a weird thing—getting cremated. I hope I just spontaneously combust because I don't like any of the options. . . . When Mr. P was crying, it made me wonder why anyone bothers loving somebody else. (I don't really mean that, but I feel it.)

POSTCARD

Fred Kelly

I pulled Fred's license plate CD case out of my backpack. I flipped through the pages of liner notes and CDs, shining the light on the album covers. There were his favorite classic-rock albums, but near the end was the Miles Davis album that Fred bought in Harvard Square, with the storm brewing on the cover. On the next page, there was an album called *Head Hunters* by Herbie Hancock. The cover art showed a yellow robot-like character playing a keyboard with his band behind him. I had no idea when or where Fred had bought it.

I popped the Miles Davis CD into my Discman and leaned against the door. It sounded like the same music that Fred had been playing along with, the night I watched him from my window. I tried to listen for what Fred had heard, but by the time the trumpet came in, I was done.

I sat up and looked at Mr. Patterson.

"You like jazz," I said.

"What?" He seemed a little dazed, like he'd been half asleep. "Yes. Yes, I do like jazz."

"Do you like this?" I said, stretching the earphones over his head. I restarted the first track and watched his face for clues—the wrinkles in his brow, his squinty eyes.

"No, I can't say that I care for it," he said loudly. Sookie looked in the rearview mirror. "Who is it?"

"Miles Davis."

"Yes, his work got a little strange in the seventies."

I took back the earphones.

"Do *you* like it?" Mr. Patterson asked.

I shook my head. "Fred liked it . . . I think."

"Maybe you have to see it performed live to appreciate it." Mr. Patterson shrugged. "And maybe you don't have to like it, but you keep your mind open to it. You trust that Mr. Davis knows what he's doing."

I nodded.

I switched the CDs and put the yellow robot in the Disc-man. The farty bass filled my brain. I liked the rhythm right away, and I knew that it was the song that Fred had danced to in his bug-eyed glasses. I could see his ridiculous moves and the smile on his face. My chest began to feel tight and tears leaked down my cheeks.

Mr. Patterson covered my hand with his.

I was never going to look out my window and see Fred dance again. And I would never have fifty more years with my mom, whom everyone seemed to know better than I did. I closed my eyes and focused on the cymbal taps.

I woke up with my head against the window and pulled off the headphones. I closed my eyes again, already half asleep when I heard Sookie say quietly, "How's Lucy doing?"

Dad breathed in through his nose and shook his head. "Well, she ate dinner last night and breakfast today, so that seemed good. But maybe I gotta work harder on getting her out of the house. Getting her mind on something else. Trouble is, she used to do everything with Fred. I mean everything."

"But she's not sittin' around the house. It was her idea to go to Maine. And she's been tryin' to figure out Helen's paper. And she learned how to gut fish. That's doing somethin'."

"I guess so," Dad said.

"How are you doing on the couch?" Sookie asked.

"What?"

"What's it like going from being a workaholic to this?"

Dad hesitated. I kept my eyes closed.

"Well, I hate it," Dad said. "When I was keeping busy, I didn't worry so much about the things I couldn't fix. Now I lie around and the sharks make me think of Helen. And my foot makes me think of Fred. And Fred makes me think of how easily it could have been Lucy who drowned."

It was quiet for a long time. The car moved past the lights of a highway rest stop, breaking the darkness a couple of times.

"You know what Helen would say?" Sookie asked.

"What?"

"Don't resist pain," Sookie said.

My eyes were wide-open.

"What?" I asked, sitting up.

Dad looked over his shoulder. "How long have you been awake?" he asked.

"A while," I said. "Who wants pain?"

"Uh, no one. But when you feel sad or angry or afraid, let yourself feel it," Sookie said. "That's all she meant."

"Don't try to turn it off," Dad added.

"Oh. When did she tell you that?" I tapped Sookie on the head.

"I don't know. A few times, I guess," Sookie said. "Probably when my dog died. When I got divorced. When my dad drove the boat into the side of a bridge."

"I've been feeling pain all summer," I said. "Now what?"

"Yeah, now what?" Dad said.

Sookie looked at Dad and shrugged. "I don't know!"

"Adapt!" Mr. Patterson yelled. "Adjust!"

I thought he was asleep. He closed his eyes again, and in a minute, I could hear him breathing, his head against the back shelf of the Diplomat. I dragged my backpack out of the darkness, onto my lap and slowly pulled the zipper. I took out the flashlight and Mom's research proposal and flipped to the section where she explains how the fisherman would tag the shark. As usual, my eyes zeroed in on the pictures. There was a crude outline of an adult male on the pulpit of a harpoon boat. He had no features, like a homicide chalk drawing, and he was facing me, instead of showing his profile and going after the great whites like he was supposed to be doing. I got this devilish feeling and I picked up a pencil and started filling in Sookie's features. I gave him a pair of Oakley sunglasses and a four-day-old beard. I drew a tank top and a pair of waders like he wore on the boat. I put a Moxie can beside him on the pulpit. I wrote Sookie above his head and made an arrow, in case there was any question. Part of me looked down in horror at how I'd defaced Mom's work, but the other part of me giggled. If I was going to be the census taker, then this was my research paper and I could give Sookie a farmer's tan if I wanted to.

I blew some eraser dust off the paper and into the dark. Sure enough, there was the spotter plane that we'd all talked about in Vern's study, the one that was going to locate the sharks for the fisherman to tag. Vern Devine wasn't talking crazy at all.

27. Dr. Robin Walker

A COUPLE OF DAYS WENT BY WITHOUT A REPLY FROM
Fred—no kayak-chasing sharks or unmistakable fins in the
newspaper. It was possible that I would have taken anything as a message from Fred, like a new *Jaws* T-shirt in the
window at the Chinese imports shop, or a cartoon shark
pushing a lawnmower on the side of a landscaping trailer. It
didn't have to be a real, live one. I just wanted a sign.

I brought my sketch pad and backpack upstairs to
Mom's office and plopped everything on the floor beside
her desk. I opened up the windows to let the breeze in and
blow out the smell of old air and silverfish. At the desk, I
flipped through the drawings, looking at all the sketches
of shark parts—fins, teeth, and vertebrae. It was August.
School was creeping up in a few weeks. If I was going to
finish the Great White Shark page, so I could pass in the
field guide to Ms. Solomon, I needed to get down to business. But when I looked at the sketch pad, all I had were
puzzle pieces of the shark, when I needed to have a complete portrait.

I gnawed on my eraser.

I pulled Mom's research proposal out of my bag and
opened to the page where I'd given Mom's fisherman a

beard and a can of Moxie. I giggled at how ridiculous it looked. Then, I looked from left to right on the desktop.

My dorsal fin sketches.

Her tagging drawings.

My dorsal fin sketches.

Her tagging drawings.

It was eerie how close my work had become to hers.

Everything on Mom's desk had been pretty much untouched. In fact, there was a layer of dust on the lamp, the Rolodex, and the stapler. I moved our work to the floor, took off my sock, and started dusting everything. When I couldn't get all of the dirty bits, I grabbed a damp washcloth and a dry one from the bathroom and went over the desk again.

I put everything back on the desktop where it had been before, but when I set down the Rolodex, the mini-filing cabinet with all of the names of people she knew and worked with, it flopped open to a name. ROBIN WALKER.

Her business card was stapled to the Rolodex card. It was clearly outdated since it didn't say, *Dr.* Robin Walker. I wondered if Robin knew anything about the tags. I dialed the number.

"Cat Cove Marine Laboratory. This is Robin."

"Hi, Dr. Walker," I said. "This is Lucy Everhart. Helen Everhart's daughter. Did you used to work—"

"Lucy!" she said. "How are you?"

"Doing okay," I said. "How 'bout you?"

"No complaints. To what do I owe this honor?" she asked.

"What?"

"What can I do for you?"

"Uh, I found one of Mom's research proposals. The one called, 'Proposal for Cape Cod White Shark and Gray Seal Study.'"

There was a pause.

"I *know* the one you are talking about," said Robin.

I felt a layer of sweat break out on my upper lip.

"I've been trying to figure it out," I said. "I get that the spotter plane sees the shark in the water and the fisherman tags the shark with a harpoon, but can you tell me how the tags work?"

"Sure," she said. I could tell from her voice that she was surprised that I was asking. "They're acoustic tags. Acoustic tags use sonar. Each tag has a transmitter that sends sound pulses into the water," Robin said. "So when a tagged shark swims within a couple of hundred meters of the hydrophone, it makes a *ping*."

There was a lot of technical vocabulary flying around, but I wanted to make sense of what she was saying, so I just kept asking questions.

"Can you actually hear the pings?" I said.

"Not with human ears, but the system that we helped design mixes the signal with another frequency of sound, so you can hear the pings through a set of headphones. And to follow a shark, you follow its pings."

"That's crazy!" I said.

"And each tag is set at a different frequency, so you can differentiate between the sharks."

"What?" I said.

"Each tag has its own special ping," said Robin.

"So each shark with a tag makes its own noise?" I asked.

"Basically," she said.

I pictured sharks in the ocean, calling out their own names as they swam by.

"We've been trying to build and fund the equipment for years," Robin said. "But it's happening, Lucy. We hope to tag our first sharks by the end of the summer."

"What?" I said. "This is happening?"

"Oh, it's happening," she said.

"Wow," I said. "Were you one of the biologists who worked with Mom and Vern on the study?"

"Yes, I worked with your mom on that project. We all miss her. It took Ray and me a long time to be able to envision moving forward without her."

I smiled. "Is Ray another biologist?"

"Yes," she said.

"We've been seeing the sharks in the news," I said. "We even had one in Rockport."

"Sookie's shark," she said. "I know. Ray and I were stuck at a conference. We wanted to do a necropsy on that one."

"I forgot that you know Sookie," I said, looking down at the bearded fisherman standing in the pulpit in Mom's proposal.

Robin sighed. "We've been calling him for a while, hoping that he would follow through and be our tagger, our captain. But it's okay. We have a couple of other leads."

"You called him recently?" I asked.

"Over the winter," said Robin. "He was good friends with your mother for a very long time. I think he was genuinely interested in the project, but I think it was mostly a big favor to your mom."

"Why are you tagging them?" I asked. "What kind of information can you get?"

"We can tag the sharks and maybe, while they come here to eat, we can keep an eye on them to figure out why they do what they do. Figure out how many are coming to the area and who's returning."

"The census," I said. I told Robin about going to visit Vern, how he thought I was my mom and told me to keep collecting data.

"That's exactly what we're doing," she said.

"And the fisherman aims the harpoon at the shark and the shark is tagged?" I asked.

"Yes. It's tricky work. The shark is a moving target and you really need to get that tag right at the sweet spot at the base of the dorsal fin."

"It doesn't hurt the shark?" I asked.

"It shouldn't," she said. "We've been tagging other types of fish for years with no negative effects."

I looked down at the desk.

My dorsal fin sketches.

Her tagging drawings.

"It's funny," I said. "I didn't pay much attention to Mom's work when she was here. She was just my mom. But since Sookie's shark, something is different. I'm working on a project for school. I've been spending a lot of my time drawing shark parts in my sketchbook. Trying to figure out how they work."

"That's pretty much what I do every day," she said.

"Right."

"You went all the way to Maine to ask Vern about the study?" she asked.

"Yeah."

"Wow," she said. "If you have any other questions, call me anytime."

"Thanks," I said.

"And if you see Sookie, tell him we pay big money."

"You do?" I asked.

She laughed. "Not really."

After I hung up with Robin, I ran downstairs to tell Dad what I'd learned about the tags and the pings. He was on one crutch, sifting through the mail on the kitchen table.

"Hey, Dad," I began.

But he interrupted and extended a postcard to me. It was the photo of Miles Davis wearing the bug-eyed glasses from Fred's bulletin board. My heart was beating triple time, waiting to see who'd sent it.

Hi Lucy,

I was in Fred's room today and I saw this on his wall. It reminded me of the day we went into Harvard Square. I couldn't believe he bought those glasses. So weird. One minute Mom and Bridget and I are bribing him to take showers and the next minute he's asking Mom if he can buy his own clothes for school. Fred didn't care about that stuff. Did he?

How was your road trip? Mr. Patterson behave himself?

Fiona

POSTCARD

Lucy Everhart

6 Smith Street

Rockport MA, 01966

"Who's it from?" Dad asked.

"Fiona," I said, still thinking about her question. She was right. Fred had never cared about what he looked like. He'd rather get ten more minutes of sleep than shower before school.

"Was Fred acting weird to you?" I asked. "Over the summer?"

Dad scrunched his lips together. "I don't think so, but you'd know better."

I made a fart noise with my mouth. I had no clue.

I ran upstairs and stuck the postcard to my bulletin board, Miles's face looking out with a deep crease in his forehead above his nose. I could barely see his eyes through the glasses, but he looked annoyed.

28. Gin Rummy

THE NEXT MORNING, I FED TWO POSTCARDS INTO THE mailbox outside of the bookstore. One was wearing a stamp and the other was unstamped. I stood there making a wish to Fred. *Send me a shark, will you? A real one this time.*

I closed the door and was about to pedal back home, when Mr. Scanlon, the school adjustment counselor, walked out of the bookstore. He was a short man with a light-brown mustache. He wore a summery button-down shirt and sandals—and while I had never seen Jimmy Buffett before, I imagined this was what he looked like. Mr. Scanlon had a brown paper bag under his arm. He turned toward the side that was opposite of the mailbox and I could have slipped away undetected, except that I called out, "Hi, Mr. Scanlon."

He looked over his shoulder and walked back toward me, surprised.

"Lucy?" he asked, unsure of my name. Good Lord, I thought everybody in town knew who I was. Maybe he was just spacey with faces.

"Yup," I said.

"Nice to meet you."

He put out his hand and looked at me with a furrowed brow. "You're at the top of my list for the fall."

"For what?" I said, shaking his small hand.

"To talk."

"About what?"

"Whatever you'd like." And he said it really sincerely, which made me feel like a jerk.

"Well, you want to talk now?" I asked, shrugging.

"Sure," he said.

"There's a bench at the bottom of the hill," I said, leading him down to the landing beside the bookstore that overlooked Front Beach. I ditched my bike and took a seat.

"How are you doing today?" he asked.

"Okay," I said. "Today feels okay."

Mr. Scanlon looked at me with a calm face. Counselors and therapists were always comfortable with eye contact and long stretches of awkward silence. I wasn't, probably because I didn't know this guy and probably because he was waiting for me to unload the horrors of the summer. We sat for a few moments in total quiet.

"What did you want to talk about?" he asked.

"Nothing really," I said.

"Do you want to play cards?" he asked.

"You brought cards?"

"Hmm-mmm," he said, pulling a pack from his back pocket.

"Sure," I said. I scooted to the edge and he shuffled the cards against the granite bench.

"What do you want to play?" he asked. "Garbage? War?"

"How 'bout gin rummy?" I asked.

He looked up at me and smiled. "Who taught you how to play gin rummy?"

"My neighbor, Mr. Patterson."

Mr. Scanlon nodded and he cut the deck.

"Have you known Mr. Patterson a long time?"

"Like, forever," I said. "He is pretty old. Maybe ninety."

Mr. Scanlon nodded and dealt us ten cards apiece. "What's he like?"

"He's a good guy. He sits on his porch a lot in his undershirt, listening to a police scanner. Which is a little weird, but I like it because he's always there if I need anything. He still plays the French horn with the American Legion band on Sunday nights."

I picked up my cards and fanned them out in my palm, grouping the queens together and ordering a run of hearts. Mr. Scanlon took a card from the stockpile and placed it faceup on the bench. Four of clubs.

"You can go first," he said.

I shrugged and took another card from the stockpile.

"Why do counselors always play games with kids?" I asked, discarding a jack.

"I guess we're not very original," he said. "Have you played gin rummy with another counselor before?"

"No, but I used to play Memory with the elementary school counselor, Ms. Watts. When I was little."

He nodded, picking up another card and putting it in the discard pile.

"You know my mom died, right?" I asked.

"Yes," he said. "How old were you?"

"Seven," I said, picking up the fourth queen. "She had a brain aneurysm. She went fast."

"I'm sorry," he said, looking up from his cards. "That must have been very hard."

"It was," I said. "But I don't think I need to talk about that."

"No? What do you need to talk about?" he asked.

"Fred," I said. "The accident."

"Okay," Mr. Scanlon said.

There was another pause in conversation. I chose a three of spades from the stockpile and discarded it. Mr. Scanlon picked it up and put down an ace.

"I have a question," I said.

"Sure," he said.

I let out a breath and picked up another heart. He picked up my trash and slipped it into his hand. "Go ahead."

I took a five of diamonds from the stockpile and slid it beside a five of spades in my hand. "I've been writing post-cards to Fred."

"Since he passed away?" Mr. Scanlon asked.

"Yup," I said.

"Tell me about it," he said, looking at me with a half smile.

"Well, things pop into my head during the day. Things I used to save for Fred."

"Like what?" He turned over a card and it went straight to the discard pile.

"Jokes. Things I see," I said. "I just mailed him a card. I told him I spoke to a biologist about tagging white sharks. And that I thought I heard someone's inhaler puff when I rode by the bus stop and I almost fainted."

His eyes narrowed, quizzically.

"Fred had asthma. The noise made me think he was here."

Mr. Scanlon nodded. "And you felt panicked?"

"Yeah, when I realized it wasn't him."

Mr. Scanlon nodded deeper, almost like a shallow bow.

"Anyway, I write these thoughts on postcards and drop them into a mailbox."

"Do you expect to get a reply?" he asked.

"No," I said, which was sort of a lie. "I just like writing them."

"Was there a question you had about the postcards?" he asked.

"Yeah," I said. "Is there something wrong with writing them?"

I picked up the five of hearts and said, "Gin!"

Mr. Scanlon spread his cards on the bench.

"Not bad," I said.

Mr. Scanlon rested his elbows on his knees and half

smiled again. "I think you'll write postcards until you don't feel like writing postcards anymore and that's okay. There is nothing wrong with sending postcards to Fred," he said.

"Mr. Scanlon?" I said, my stomach flipping. I wanted to leave it alone, but I had to know if I was not okay.

"Yes?"

"I kind of pretend that every great white that I see on the news or read about in the paper is a message from Fred to me. I know wherever he is, he probably can't talk to me, but I'm not ready to deal with that. Am I crazy?"

He looked out at the ocean.

"From what I've heard from the staff, it seems like your friendship with Fred was devoted and meaningful. It will take some time to get used to him not being here," he said.

"'Devoted and meaningful.' What does that mean?" There was an edge in my voice, but I didn't care.

"I'm sorry," he said. "I don't know either of you well. And certainly not well enough to try to describe your relationship."

"I don't know how to describe it either," I said.

"Do you want to talk more about that?"

"I'm not sure what to say. Up until recently, I thought I knew everything there was to know about Fred. Then this summer, there were just all these new things. Fred growing his hair, listening to different music, jumping in the quarry." I pulled the necklace out of my shirt. "And this."

Mr. Scanlon studied the pendant and, then, my face.

"I get that our friendship was meaningful, but I'm so confused as to what it *meant* in the end."

He nodded. It was just quiet for a bit.

"Maybe writing to him will actually help you figure out your *own* feelings. And maybe he *is* talking to you through sharks. Who am I to tell you you're wrong?"

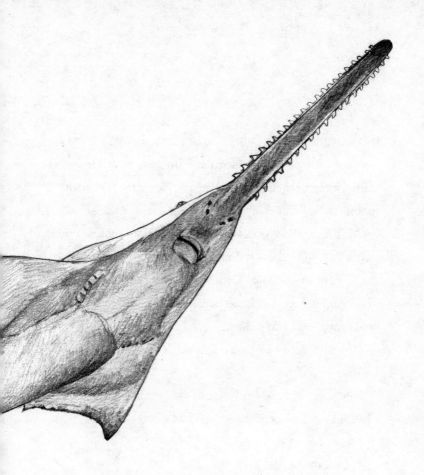

29. *Lobster Dinner*

DAD HAD REACHED THE POINT WITH HIS CAST WHERE IT WAS more of an itchy annoyance than anything else. He had started sleeping in his bedroom again. He cleaned the bathroom, cooked dinner, and even cut the grass. Since he still couldn't drive, Sookie got into the habit of airing him out once a day. When he was done fishing, Sookie drove Dad to the IGA, to the Building Center, or wherever Dad wanted to go. And if there was something in it for me, like gummies or art supplies, I came along.

One day, we drove by Bass Rocks, and Dad said, "Pull over for a sec."

Sookie parked the truck on the side of the windy road, and Dad looked out at the waves.

"What are we doing here?" I asked.

"Just looking," he said.

I realized he was watching the dive flags bobbing on the surface, missing one of his old spots. There were only a couple of things he couldn't do with a cast: drive and get wet. Not being able to get wet was a problem for Dad. He liked to quote JFK, who apparently said once that the percentage of salt in our blood is the same as what's in the ocean and because of this connection we always come back to the sea.

That was my parents, exactly.

∘ ∘ °∘

One night, Dad asked me to peel potatoes for dinner.

"That's a lot of potatoes," I said, looking at about five pounds of dirty stones on the counter. "What are we going to do with all this?"

The doorbell rang and Dad called, "Can you get that?"

"Fine," I said.

Sookie stood in the doorway, holding a Styrofoam chest with a six-pack of Moxie on top.

"Where'd you get the Moxie?" I asked.

"Cumberland Farms!" he said, as though it was unheard of. Dad took the six-pack and led Sookie into the kitchen.

"What's in the cooler?" I said.

"Dinner."

Sookie stopped and lifted the lid, presenting a pile of crustaceans, writhing like leggy bugs.

"Lobster!" I cried. "I didn't know you were coming over."

"It was a last-minute invitation," he said.

Lobster had always been one of the meals that my dad had prepared on his own. He'd put on a wet suit and go scavenging off Back Beach, bringing home lobster in his mesh bag. He'd boil them in the large pot that was used only for this occasion. At the table, Mom and Dad would dissect them with precision, leaving no meat to waste. They'd drop the soft claws and tails into my bowl of melted butter, as though they were feeding the queen. Even after Mom died, there had always been lobster dinners in the summer, though this summer had been different.

Looking into Sookie's cooler, I thought about the choking factor of the rubbery meat, but lobster was one of my favorite meals. There had to be a way to get it down. Sookie replaced the lid and hefted the cooler onto the counter.

"Given any more thought to tagging sharks with Robin?" I asked. I had already bothered him about it twice that week.

He nodded. Looked me in the eye and said, "No."

"She said it pays big bucks," I said, knowing that Robin was being sarcastic.

"What do I need money for?"

I thought of Sookie rubbing a stack of scratch tickets in Mr. Patterson's car and I shrugged. The screen door bounced closed again and I walked back to the foyer to see who it was.

"Hello, Lucy," said Mr. Patterson.

"What the heck is going on?" I asked.

"It's a dinner party. Your manners are lacking."

"Are you surprised?" I asked.

In the kitchen, Sookie handed Mr. Patterson a can.

"Oh, goody!" Mr. Patterson said, cracking open the Moxie.

"I'll get the knife," I said to Dad, eyeing the cooler.

There was a time when Dad used to throw the live lobster in the pot, potentially suffering a horrible, slow death. But shortly before my mom had died, Fred had come over for dinner one night. And he'd spoken up.

"Tom," Fred had said. "Could you kill the lobster *before* you cook it?

Dad had looked at Fred for a moment. "I cook lobster the way my mom did," he finally said, holding the lobster, and he'd gestured like he was going to throw it into the pot.

Fred moved closer to Dad and the squirming shellfish.

"Let me do it," he said, reaching over the top of the writhing legs for the body.

We all watched Fred carry the active lobster over to the silverware drawer, like it was as lifeless as an eggplant. Even though there had been rubber bands around the claws, I would have never picked it up. Fred slid open the drawer. He pulled out a large knife.

"What are you doing there, buddy?" Mom asked.

Dad looked at Mom and shook his head. Mom looked at Fred and stretched out her hands.

"Okay, we'll take care of it," she said.

Fred passed her the lobster and the knife. From then on, Dad never boiled a lobster alive. At least not in front of me.

One by one, he pulled the lobsters out of the cooler, and laid them out on the cutting board. *BAM*.

I washed the pencil off my hands at the sink, so I didn't have to look.

"Why do you bother with that?" Sookie yelled over the noise. "It ain't necessary."

Dad didn't answer.

"Getting ready for school, Lucy?" Mr. Patterson asked, taking a sip of Moxie.

"No. I have three weeks left," I said. "But I did play gin rummy with the school shrink the other day and I beat him."

"I told you those skills would come in handy," Mr. Patterson said.

The doorbell rang. Dad beat me to it. I heard him say her name before I saw her small frame.

"Maggie," he said. "Come in."

Fred's mom entered the house, in her usual uniform— sweatshirt and shorts. She looked small and pale, a little greasy. Her brow furrowed, and she smiled a complicated smile when our eyes met. There was a shoebox under her arm.

Maggie heard voices in the kitchen. "I didn't know you had company. I just wanted to talk to Lucy for a minute."

Dad and I exchanged glances. I shrugged to let him know it was okay with me.

"Come in," he said again. "I'll check on the lobster."

"Fancy," said Maggie.

I walked her into the living room. She settled beside me on the couch and rested the shoebox on her knees. "How have you been?" she asked.

"Okay. Today was a good day."

"Oh?"

"I worked on the field guide. I'm having lobster for dinner."

"That's good," she said. Her brow was still creased.

"How have you been?" I asked.

She rolled her eyes. "I've been better."

"What's in there?" I asked, remembering Fred and the birds, toads, and mice I'd seen him carry in shoeboxes.

Without a word, she lifted the lid, revealing a heap of postcards. I saw the Japanese wood block of the ocean waves and shifted the loose stack with my fingertips. There were loons and moose and a few I had picked up in town. My own handwriting marked every card. I hadn't given much thought to where the cards would actually end up. At the worst, maybe they'd land in a wastebasket at the post office. But Maggie ending up with the postcards was such an obvious conclusion.

"I wrote these to Fred," I confessed.

"I know."

"How did you get them?"

"The postmaster delivered the stack. He wasn't sure what to do with them. They were all unsigned."

I put my face in my hands and cried. Maggie hooked her arm around me and pressed my head into her chest.

"Did you read them?" I asked.

"Most of them. I'm sorry, Lucy. I couldn't help it. Did you think he would write you back?"

"No." But I thought he'd been sending me sharks.

I dragged my arm across my wet nose. "I just had all these things to say to him and he wasn't there. I didn't know where to put those ideas. I need to keep talking to him. I need to feel like he's still there."

She rubbed my back. "I *get* it. One morning last week, I went into his room to wake him up." Then Maggie started to cry. "Don't feel bad about sending postcards. That's a lot healthier than the way I cope."

"I ran into the school counselor in town," I said. "I think I'm gonna see more of him in the fall."

"My girls would be so happy if I saw someone," she said in a flat voice, meaning that she hadn't been to grief counseling.

"I kind of like the idea of having a place in school where I can be honest about feeling bad."

"I'm happy you'll have that," she said, rubbing my back again. I was glad she was there. When my mom died, I remember Maggie teaching my dad how to do my hair. I remember her being nearby all of the time. It had been different with Fred's death because we both felt lost.

"Your back feels bony. Have you lost weight?" she asked.

"Yeah, not intentionally," I said.

"No, me neither," she said. "What's that around your neck?"

I put my hand to my chest and realized that the pendant had popped out from inside my shirt. I was afraid she might take it away. I still didn't know whose it was.

"Wow," Maggie said, sliding a fingertip over the mermaid. "It's very old. And it's real gold. Is that dental floss?"

I shrugged.

"You need a stronger chain," she said. She paused a moment before continuing: "How did he give it to you?"

"He didn't," I said. "I'm not even sure it's mine."

"It's yours," said Maggie. "It's a meaningful gift."

"But what does it *mean*?" I practically yelled.

"Ask Mr. Patterson," she said. "He can give you the full story."

"You know the story?" I asked, searching her face.

"Ask Mr. Patterson," she repeated.

I wanted to burst into the kitchen and interrogate him right then, but Maggie pulled a postcard out of the shoebox. The Twin Lights. "There is one of these that I can't stop thinking about."

Twin Lights/Thatchers Island, Rockport, MA
Photo credit: Zoe Adler

Your mom wants to blame Lester. I wish we never went in the water that night. Then you'd still be here.

Lester told me he'd trade places with you in a heartbeat.

POSTCARD

Fred Kelly

"I just wish he were here," I sobbed.

Dad must have heard me crying because he came through the swinging door from the kitchen and was standing in the living room.

"It was an unfortunate accident," Maggie said.

"Then why do you blame Lester?" I cried.

There was silence for a moment. Maggie looked worn-out.

Dad walked over on one crutch and took a seat across from the couch.

"Maggie, don't you remember?" he said, like he was coaxing a memory from someone he loved. "Don't you remember when you and Helen, and Sookie and me used to go to the quarries in the summertime. We'd swim and lie around, listening to music. Sookie would say crazy things and make us laugh."

Maggie sniffed. "Yes."

"We'd go up at night and there were thousands of stars. And every once in a while, one of us would get ahold of a few skunky cans of beer or some Thunderbird—"

"That was different," Maggie interrupted. "We were stupid."

"We were stupid," Dad said. "And sometimes we went swimming after we drank. And nothing bad ever happened."

"We were lucky," Maggie said.

"We were lucky," he said. "People do stupid things sometimes. And every once in a while, something terrible happens because of it."

Maggie was crying hard and I rubbed her back. I couldn't stop looking at my dad.

"Me, you, Lester, Lucy. We're all good people who have done stupid things. We have to look out for one another, Maggie. Rescue each other even," he said. "You know how to do that better than anyone."

Through my palm, I could feel Maggie take a deep breath.

"It's nobody's fault. Or it's everybody's fault. But the kids need us. Lester too," Dad said.

"I know," she said.

"You want to stay for lobster?" I asked.

"No thanks, dear." She looked at me, cradled both of my cheeks in her hands, and kissed my forehead. "Thank you."

Dad left his crutch on the ground. He walked slowly toward Maggie and put his arms around her. She sobbed into his chest and he squeezed tighter.

"Want me to walk you home?" I asked.

"No, I think I'll make it," she said.

When Maggie left, Dad returned to the kitchen. I sat on the couch, looking at the box of postcards, wondering what to do with them. I left the box on the coffee table and walked into the kitchen.

"What did Maggie want?" Sookie asked.

"Nothing," I said, feeling dizzy from Maggie's visit, the pendant, and the shoebox. I stood behind my chair and pulled the necklace out from under my shirt.

"What *is* this?" I asked, my voice cracking.

Everyone looked up at me, as though I sounded a little crazy. Mr. Patterson squinted and frowned.

"What in God's name is that pendant hanging from?" he said.

I touched the gold charm.

"Dental floss," I said loudly.

"Are you nuts? That's eighteen-karat gold!"

"I don't even know what the heck it IS?" I yelled, pulling on the necklace and stomping my foot. "I found a box in Fred's backpack, so I opened it and found THIS thing. Maggie said to ask you about it! She said it was a *meaningful* gift! Everyone says that about me and Fred—that there was this deep MEANING. Why can't anyone tell me what the MEANING was?!"

My cheeks were burning. I was crying. I kept pulling on the necklace, trying to break the dental floss, but it wouldn't split. Dad pushed his chair away from the table. I knew he was going to try to settle me down, but everything was bubbling up.

"Somebody else's old piece of junk!" I yelled.

I ripped the necklace over my head and threw it at the wall. It bounced off a doorframe and landed with a *thunk* in a pan of melted butter.

Mr. Patterson gasped.

I crumpled into my chair, sobbing.

"Sookie, can you take care of that?" Dad asked, nodding his head toward the counter. He pulled up the empty seat beside me and rubbed my back. I howled with my face in my hands. *Fred is gone.*

I felt embarrassed about the box of postcards that were all dead ends, read by Maggie and unread by Fred.

I felt angry that Fred and Mom would never know me as a grown woman.

I remembered the look on Mr. Patterson's face when I said that the necklace was junk. Dad kept passing me napkins until I was dry.

Water trickled into the kitchen sink, as Sookie degreased the necklace. When he was finished, he returned to the table with the necklace wrapped in a dish towel and handed me the bundle.

"Thanks," I said. I unwrapped the pendant and turned it over a couple of times. It looked the same, intact from its flight across the kitchen. The dental floss was wet, but not greasy.

Mr. Patterson spoke very quietly. "Fred came over one day and asked how I got Mrs. Patterson to be my girlfriend. I laughed and I said, 'Is this about Lucy?' and he nodded."

My heart sped up. I wiped my face and looked at Mr. P.

"So I suggested he give you a gift—a piece of jewelry. He said he didn't have that kind of money, so I gave him the key to Mrs. Patterson's jewelry box."

He took a sip of Moxie.

"I tried to help him choose something. I offered a ring,

some ivory hair combs. Fred thought those were cruel to elephants and put them back into the box. He passed up diamonds and a garnet necklace before he settled on that one." Mr. Patterson pointed at the pendant. "The mermaid caught his eye. I told him it was a mechanical pencil. He was very excited about that discovery. He said it was 'the right gift for Lucy.'"

"It's a *what*?" I whispered.

"It's an Art Nouveau mechanical pencil. I bought it for Mrs. Patterson ages ago. She used to wear it around her neck."

A mechanical pencil. I picked it up to see how the pencil worked, but I couldn't figure it out. My hands were shaking a little.

Mr. Patterson put out his hand. I dropped it into his palm. He twisted the barrel. Oily water dripped out the bottom. "There's still lead in it, though you might need to dry it out inside," he said, handing it back to me. "Fred thought you could use it for your art."

I looked down at the pencil. On my napkin, I drew loopy squiggles and wrote my name. The lead was soft and good for drawing.

"Get yourself a proper chain, will you? Mrs. Patterson's broke ages ago, and it was made of a stronger material than dental floss."

"It's triple looped," I said in a quiet voice.

"Lucy," said Mr. Patterson.

"I'm sorry," I said, looking at Mr. Patterson.

"It's okay, dear," he said.

"Can I see it again?" Sookie asked, looking at the pendant. I passed it to Sookie.

"I still don't understand," I said. "Why did he want to give it to *me*?"

"You were his favorite person in the world and he wanted to tell you," Mr. Patterson said. He reached into his pocket, pulled out a handkerchief, and pressed it into each eye. "That's what it means."

I knew he was thinking about Mrs. Patterson. And that's when it hit me. I'd always suspected that I was Fred's favorite person in the whole world. And he was mine. But neither of us had ever said that out loud. Not to each other. I shivered, thinking that he had wanted to say it to me. It was like standing on the edge of the quarry again.

30. *Stronger*

I STARTED TO WRITE FRED A POSTCARD, BUT THERE WERE too many words for the small space, so I wrote him a letter instead. I told him about the butter fiasco and asked him when he'd planned on giving me the necklace. The last words were *I keep hoping I'll hear you chuck rocks at my window and ask me to go somewhere with you.* Then I stuffed the letter into an envelope and put it in my pocket.

A car door slammed outside and I looked out the window. In the porch light of Fred's house, I saw Lester heading up Fred's walkway. He rang the bell. A shadow drew toward the screen door and Maggie appeared. They stood for what seemed like a long time, exchanging words, separated by the screen. And then Maggie invited Lester into the house.

I breathed out through my mouth, hoping that the talk would go well.

And then something bounced off the side of my house. I heard a rock ricochet off the trim around my window.

My heart pounded.

I pressed my face close to the screen and looked down.

Fiona was standing in the light of the streetlamp.

"Hi," I said, trying to hide my disappointment, though I was still curious as to why she wanted me.

"Hey," she said. "I got your postcard."

"Oh," I said. It had been more than a few days since I'd dropped it in the mailbox, before playing gin rummy with Mr. Scanlon.

"Maggie put it on my dresser, but I didn't see it until tonight!" she said. "Want to take a walk?"

I looked at the clock. It was after nine. "I smell like lobster," I said.

"I don't care," she said.

"I'll be right down."

She was standing at the end of my driveway, wearing a flowy dress, a sweatshirt, and the red Chinese shoes. I was wearing my blue Chinese shoes. She smiled and said, "Where do you want to go?" As if we had always taken late-night walks together.

I shrugged. "Wherever. We can just walk toward town."

We took a left at the end of our street and headed to the ocean. There was a boat far from shore that was moving slowly through the black water with white lights like stars at the mast and the front.

"I saw Lester go into your house," I said, as we walked along the railing, the beach below us.

"Yeah," she said. "He went in the front door and I went out the back."

"Are you mad at him?"

"No," she said. "I know that I should be there to make

sure my mom doesn't say anything horrible to him. But I just . . . left."

I nodded, thinking about what Fiona had said as we passed an older couple out for a walk.

"It will be okay."

"I'm not so sure," Fiona said.

"Your mom stopped by my house tonight. She talked to my dad. I think it helped."

"She talked to your dad?" Fiona repeated.

I nodded.

"That makes me feel better."

At some point, I realized that I was leading us to the mailbox, where I had deposited each of Fred's postcards throughout the summer. When we got to the bookstore, I paused in front and looked up at the three big awnings over the door and windows, the mailbox to my right.

As if Fiona wasn't going to notice, I walked over, pulled the envelope out of my pocket, and stealthily dropped it inside. I assumed that we could keep walking, but her feet were planted on the sidewalk.

"Are you sending that to Fred?" she asked.

"What?" I asked.

"I know about the shoebox. My mom says too much," she said. "And your dad doesn't say enough."

I watched her face for signs of disgust. She thought for a moment and said, "You could get a journal. Or you could talk to me."

She looked me right in the eye, like she was serious.

"You've got plenty of friends," I said. "I don't—"

"No. You're my sister," she said. "Not biologically, but better. More meaningful. I don't know."

I wanted to hug her, but I just stood there.

"I blew up at dinner tonight. And then Mr. Patterson told me that Fred had wanted to give me the necklace," I said, pulling it out from inside my shirt. "It's a mechanical pencil." I twisted the gold rod and the lead appeared. Fiona leaned in close. "It was Mrs. Patterson's."

"Mystery solved," she said. "And, as it happens . . ." Fiona dug in her pocket. "Put out your hand."

"What?" I said.

Fiona grabbed my wrist and turned my hand. Then she slowly dropped something cool into my palm. I looked down at the metal links.

"It's sterling silver. I wish I could've gotten you gold to match. But at least this one's stronger."

At first, we couldn't break the floss. Fiona gnawed through it, which was disgusting since this string had actually passed through the cracks between my teeth on several occasions and, more recently, had floated in a pan of butter.

I pulled the pendant free and Fiona threaded the silver chain through the little eye on top. Then, she stood behind me and fastened the clasp. I stuffed the dental floss into my pocket.

"Better?" she asked.

I nodded and hugged Fiona tight.

31. *Invitation*

FRED GOT IT HALF RIGHT. HE FINALLY SENT ME ANOTHER shark. It wasn't a real live one. But it was real.

In my sleep, I heard the phone ring over the dull whir of the fan. Waking up to a phone call at dawn was more jarring than an alarm clock interrupting my dream. My dad had regularly received strange calls from work at all hours of the night, but that had stopped after the accident. I was out of practice and was dying to know who was on the phone.

I lifted my head off the pillow to uncover both ears, but the white noise muffled the sound of Dad's voice. I put both feet on the floor, flipped off the fan, and walked to the doorway.

"Where?" Dad asked.

There was a long pause. I rubbed my eyes and yawned.

"What makes you think she'd want to see that?" Dad said.

"See what?" I wondered. There was another lull on Dad's end of the call.

"You can talk to her about it," he finally said.

When the squeaking from his crutch came closer, I knew that he'd been talking about me. Dad stopped at the doorway and covered the receiver with his hand.

"It's Sookie," he said. "Says a white shark washed up on

the Cape. He's wondering if you want to watch the biologists cut it open."

He extended the phone and looked at me as though he were trying to read my reaction, as if he wondered whether I was truly interested in something that most humans (other than my mom) would find disgusting. I also wondered if it bothered him that Sookie knew something about me that he didn't.

Eyes wide, I took the phone from his hand.

"Hello?"

"It's Sookie. Sorry to wake you up," he said.

I shook my head. "No problem."

"I got a call from Robin. She said that a runner found a white shark. Washed up in Chatham. She and Ray are driving down to the beach for the necropsy," he said. "She thought you'd like to watch. That you might want to bring your sketchbook."

"I would," I said without hesitation. Dad's brow lifted slightly, like he was surprised. Even I couldn't believe that I wanted to go. I covered the receiver.

"Is that okay?" I whispered to Dad.

He nodded. "Just stay with Sookie."

"Do you want to come?" I asked.

"I don't know how I'd get around the beach with this thing. Too much sand," he said, gesturing to his foot. "But you go."

I put the phone up to my ear again.

"I'll come by in a bit," Sookie said.

"Sookie?" I said. "Why did Robin call *you*?"

"She's on my case about the tagging project," he said. "Just like you."

"Are you going to do it?" I asked.

"No comment."

Sookie's tone was so flat, I couldn't tell if he was considering it at all.

"See you soon," I said. "Thanks."

I pressed the button to end the call and crossed my arms.

"You're really up for this?" Dad asked.

"Are you that surprised?"

"Given the way this summer's going, no," he said. "You're gonna need some money for the trip."

He went looking for his wallet and returned with two twenties.

"What's this?" I asked.

"Tolls, food. Just bring me the change."

"Thanks, Dad."

I took the money.

"Bring a sweatshirt," he said. "It might be cool on the beach."

Then, as if driven by a motor, I ran downstairs to the kitchen sink and pulled out a heavy-duty garbage bag and a roll of duct tape from the junk drawer. I ran back upstairs.

"What are you doing?" he asked, as I bagged his cast.

"You need to come with us," I said.

I wrapped him up like a futuristic, ninja mummy.

"No sand'll get in there," I said. "You're getting this thing off soon anyway."

"I'll come," he said, smiling.

"Bring your camera."

He nodded.

I gathered up my art supplies and found clothes, but couldn't decide which shoes to wear to a necropsy. I thought about the scene in *Jaws* when Hooper and Chief Brody slice open the shark, releasing a river of foul, grayish fluids. I didn't want to wear anything I might ever want to wear again, so I grabbed my gym shoes.

I waited on the stoop for Sookie to arrive. Mr. Patterson was on his porch, drinking a cup of coffee, so I walked over with my backpack.

"A necropsy?" he said, making a gruesome face. "Like mother, like daughter."

I stood at the bottom of Mr. Patterson's steps.

"Don't you want to know what a huge shark looks like inside?" I asked.

"I hadn't thought about it before," he said. "But I suppose."

"You were an engineer, right?" I asked.

"Yes. A *mechanical* engineer."

"I want to know how all of the parts work, so I can draw the whole shark for my science project."

He nodded. "You're going with Sookie?"

"And Dad," I said.

I could hear Sookie's truck on Beach Street before he made either turn onto King or Smith. He pulled into my driveway, hopped down from the cab, and went into the house.

"Oh hell, I gotta see this," said Mr. Patterson.

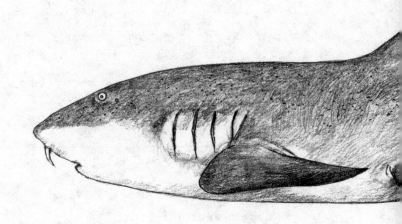

32. *Sharks Can't Digest Hair*

WALKING IN THE SAND, I SAW THE SMALL CROWD GATHERED
in an arc around the base of a rocky section of the beach,
watching the shark, the way strangers hang around, useless,
like when someone has had a seizure in a grocery store. The
shark was hung up in a huge field of boulders. I could see
glimpses of the long white belly between the bystanders.
The shark must have been the length of a swimming pool.
Sookie started to jog ahead and I felt torn between wanting
to get inside the arc right away and not wanting to leave
Dad and Mr. Patterson behind.

"You go ahead. We'll be right there," said Mr. Patterson, as if he could read my mind. I looked at Dad's boot
to make sure the duct tape was holding up. As if that cast
couldn't make his foot any hotter in August, I had to wrap
it in plastic. But when I saw Dad's face, I knew he didn't
care. With his boot in the sand and his camera around his
neck, he was home.

I ran behind Sookie, my backpack bouncing up and
down on my back, and saw an opening between two older
ladies in short terry-cloth beach dresses. I squeezed between
them, entering the arc at the edge of the rocky terrain. The
shark looked like a ghost with its white belly and broad fins

stretched to the sky, reflecting the sunlight. The head was wedged between large boulders and there was another rock between the caudal fins and tail. The shark was packed into the rocks so tightly that I wondered whether the biologists, or even the high tide, could move it.

I left the spectators at the edge of the arc and hiked into the rocks, the way Fred and I had done so many times at Folly Cove, feeling out each step before committing. I moved closer to the snout-end. The shark had taken a beating. A chunk of the nose was missing and large gashes below the injury fed into the nostrils and into the mouth. Its jaws were slightly open, showing many broken and missing teeth. I looked to the sides of the snout. I covered my nose and mouth with my hand. The smell was pungent, like opening a fridge that contained a rotting animal.

I was pretty sure this wasn't Sookie's shark that had drifted out to sea because Fred told me it would have disintegrated out there, but I had to make sure. So I hiked around the snout to the side where I thought the scar had been and I crouched in the shadow of a large fin, to see the gray side of the shark.

Sections of the gray skin had been worn away, maybe from bouncing around on the seafloor as it rolled into the beach. There was no *M*-shaped scar between the blanched-out gills and the dorsal fin. Definitely not ours. Without thinking, I put my hand where the *M* should be and Mr.

Patterson yelled from far back at the arc, "Lucy, don't touch it. You'll get worms!"

I pulled my hand away and looked up at the other spectators. One woman nodded, backing up Mr. Patterson like Mrs. Patterson would have done.

"You might want to stay back with the rest of the group down there," said a man carrying a red box, like a tool kit, toward the shark. "We don't have much time. We can't have people in the way."

I nodded, but I had no intention of moving. I watched the people wearing baseball caps, who were moving around the shark. They had brought in plastic totes, coolers, and big buckets, and deposited them in the smaller rocks just beyond the shark. One man was taking a measurement of the tail. A couple of others were talking and unloading gear. These were the biologists.

I spotted one of them, bent over a plastic tub of supplies, wearing a pair of orange waders like the ones Sookie and Lester wore on the boat. When the biologist stood up, I saw her thick, curly hair, pulled back with a purple headband. I recognized Robin right away.

She was pulling on a pair of rubber gloves as she looked at me. I was squatting next to the head, probably in her way. She smiled, as though she had known me well. She looked at Dad, Mr. Patterson, and Sookie.

"Lucy?" she asked, walking over to the snout, reaching out her gloved hand. "You made it."

I rose out of my squat and gave her my hand, like an adult would do. "Thanks for calling Sookie this morning."

"No problem," she said. "Hopefully you'll learn something here."

Sookie nearly wiped out in the rocks, but when he finally made it over, he put his hand out. "Hi, Robin. Sookie."

"It's been a long time. Nice to see you again."

"You know my dad, Tom, and that's my neighbor, Mr. Patterson," I said, pointing to them at the edge of the rocks.

"She smells a little ripe," Sookie said.

"Is she a *she*?" I asked.

"She is," said Robin.

I covered my nose and noticed fresh scrapes on Robin's arm.

"Ray, you ready?" Robin yelled. Another biologist trekked through the rocks to the shark's head.

"This is Ray Rodriguez," Robin said.

I shook hands with Ray.

Ray and Robin moved through the rocks, circling the shark, discussing types of incision. They decided on a lateral cut down the side of the fish.

"We have to move fast," she said.

"Why?" I asked.

"Tide's coming in."

I nodded. I unzipped my backpack and pulled out the sketch pad. I figured I could use it to draw and take notes, if I heard something that sounded important.

"Dad," I whispered, pointing to his camera.

He nodded.

Robin crouched down and rested a gloved hand on the shark's snout.

"Wow," she said, looking over the shark's face.

"What are those marks?" I asked.

"Some of these are scratches from a seal most likely. Maybe we'll find that seal in her gut."

I heard Vern Devine's shaky voice in my head, *Wait for the seals.*

Robin pointed to another area of the nose, near the missing chunk. "These other scrapes look like they might be from her journey to the beach."

I flipped to a clean page in the sketch pad and made a line drawing of the snout, filling in the defensive wounds from the seal in all of the right spots. I erased the section of the nose that was missing and drew a concave line.

"Robin?" I asked, blowing away eraser dust.

"Yes."

"Are you looking forward to this?"

"Absolutely."

"Why?"

"It's like opening a present. I can't wait to get the wrapper off and see what's inside."

I heard Sookie snort. He thought it sounded like Mom too.

Robin stuck her hand inside the upper jaw and nodded.

"Why are we doing this?" I asked.

"Because looking at a dead shark will tell us something about the ones that are still alive," Robin said.

o o °o

While the biologists continued to take measurements, I made a simple line drawing from nose to tail. Robin gestured for me to move closer.

"Come on in here," she said. "So you can see better."

I stood by Robin's side.

"Seeing the shark this way doesn't do her justice. They really are powerful when you see them swimming through the ocean," Robin said.

"Four-point-nine-three meters," reported Robin. I wrote the figure on my page.

Sookie and the biologists rocked the shark, moving her just slightly to help Robin take the measurements.

In the distance, the arc of onlookers grew by a few more people, and Ray walked around the shark, snapping photos with his camera. It made me think of Dad, who was standing with Mr. Patterson in the crowd.

"Ray is photographing scars, fin marks, and distinctive body markings. Though it's a little tricky with the decomposition and abrasions from knocking about in the ocean. There is a huge archive of these types of images, and biologists can use the photos to identify white sharks around the world," Robin explained.

I nodded. "I'll be right back."

I hiked back through the rocks, holding the sketch pad away from me to help keep my balance. When I got to the sand, I tucked the pad into my armpit and grabbed Mr. Patterson's elbow and Dad's hand.

"Come with me," I said. "You've gotta see this."

Mr. Patterson smiled. "This is as far as I go, dear. But thank you."

"It's not that bad," I said. "Let's just go slow."

"What if my cast gets wet?" Dad said. "I don't know."

"We'll get out of there before the tide," I said. "You can take pictures."

Dad nodded.

"I guess I'll keep an eye on Tom," Mr. Patterson said.

I tucked my sketch pad into the waistband of my shorts, stuck the pencil through my ponytail, and ferried Dad and Mr. P to the carcass. While they managed to keep their balance, I slipped on loose rock, but the sketch pad stayed dry. They took places near the dorsal fin and Dad began shooting pictures.

"How often do they eat?" I asked Robin.

"That depends. If a shark feeds on a nice seal, it may not eat again for weeks. It takes a long time for a shark to digest a large meal."

"Dorsal high—fifty-point-three," Ray called out.

I scribbled the numbers beside my drawing of the dorsal fin.

Within minutes, Ray cut the shark from the gills to the

anus and used a small knife to free the skin and muscle that covered the abdominal cavity. He pulled away a thick layer that resembled a pinkish foam carpet pad. The smell was like nervous skunks, fresh from a swim in raw sewage.

Robin made a face. "Well, her organs have seen better days. They are a little soupy. But I'm really surprised about the overall condition. It's better than I thought."

"What do you mean?" I asked.

"Well, she's been rolling around along the seafloor and it doesn't take long for isopods to get in through the gills and other openings. They feed on dead sharks from the inside out," Robin said, pulling away the skin and muscle.

That's exactly what Fred said would happen.

"Can I see the inside before you start messing around in there?" I asked, thinking of the field guide. I had been dying to know what was under the hood of this shark, so that I could draw the outside in a more realistic way.

"Sure thing," she said. "Let me make it a little easier for you."

Robin and Ray pulled back more of the carpet pad.

I drew what I saw, but without knowing what I was looking at, they were just flabby shapes. A long shape filled almost the entire cavity.

"What's that?" I asked.

"That's the liver. It can be up to twenty percent of the shark's body weight. The fatter the liver, the healthier the shark."

Was this shark healthy? Robin removed large sections of the liver and put them into plastic bins. As Ray sat one of the bins onto a scale, I peered inside. The single lobe looked like a very fat baby and there were several others to go.

"We might have better luck here," Robin said when it was time to look at the stomach contents. "The walls of the stomach are thick, so it will take them longer to break down."

The stomach was bulging, indicating that something large was inside. I drew another sketch. Once again, Robin sawed away at fine layers to make a slit down one side of the gut, which contained:

> a porpoise
>
> a toupee
>
> fish bone fragments

Dad snapped pictures. Even though the porpoise was large and essentially swallowed whole, the toupee stopped my heart.

"Pardon me, but *what is* that?" Mr. Patterson asked.

"Sharks can't digest hair," Robin said, holding up the hairball. "The shark probably ate a fur seal recently."

I was relieved that it wasn't human hair and strangely delighted that it was a seal. Mom and Vern were right.

"Hey, Robin?" I asked. "Are the seals coming back to Cape Cod?"

"Yes," she said.

"And are the white sharks following them?" I added.

"Let's talk afterward," she said, pointing the toupee at me. She held my gaze for a moment, like she knew I was on to something. I felt a shiver across my scalp.

A new brand of stink entered the atmosphere when the decaying stomach contents sat in plain view. The fish bone fragments would be sent to a lab where they could hopefully identify the specific species of fish, giving clues to the shark's whereabouts. Fred would have loved this stuff. I started a new page in my sketch pad called Stomach Contents.

Robin showed us the spiral valve of the intestines. It looked like a giant sausage link, but when Robin cut a long section from the wall, making a window into the valve, I could see a spiral structure inside, like a staircase. I thought immediately of the moon snail that Fred showed me in Folly Cove and I wondered how nature could make that perfect pattern in two different animals, for different reasons. The pattern was beautiful.

Robin pulled out the reproductive organs for a closer look and with what was salvageable of the decayed major organs packed away in coolers, the shark's carcass began to resemble the empty lobster bodies Sookie had taken away from last night's feast.

"We've got something here!" Robin cried, examining the womb on a flat rock. Her voice cracked in excitement.

Ray leaned in. There were two shark pups in the uterus, dead, of course. The shark was a mother. On the back of Stomach Contents, I drew two pups side by side.

"I have never seen pups in a white shark's uterus before," Robin told us. "This is rare."

Fred would be freaking out. Robin carefully removed them from the shark's womb and laid them on top of a cooler for a closer view. At this point, Robin and Ray seemed to forget there were several of us straining for a peek at the baby sharks and they hovered over them for a minute.

"Dad," I said, pointing at the shark pups.

∘ ∘ ° ∘

After working in the cavity for a while, Robin said, "Let's look at the gills from inside."

Robin began sawing into the shark's side with a knife. In minutes, she peeled back thick sections, like a steak, for each gill and she turned them like pages in a book. Each page had rows of red folds like an accordion made out of meat.

"These are beautiful," she said. "Lucy, will you help me?"

I looked up from sketching. "Me?"

Robin nodded and tossed me a pair of gloves, which I stretched over my fists. I left the book in the sand, and Robin motioned for me to hold one of the gill sections. I grabbed the slab. It was cold and firm. If it weren't for gutting fish on Sookie's boat, I probably would have been more grossed out. Touching the inside of the shark was fine. Smelling the inside of the shark was another story.

Robin pointed to areas of the gills while explaining to the crowd that water flows off the gills one way and blood flows the other way.

"The shark needs to swim at all times, otherwise it will suffocate."

I looked over at Sookie, who was standing on the perimeter with his arms crossed, seeming pleased with himself. I wiggled the gill flap with one hand and ran my finger over the feathery sections of the accordion. It was hard to believe how detailed all of the shark's different systems were and that I had my hand inside the body of a great white. I kept my gloves on and stayed beside Robin. When Robin cut the lens from the eye, I held it in my palm. It was perfectly round and was the color of a red grape. I touched the clear jelly that Ray squeezed from little holes in the shark's snout. The holes were actually sensory organs that gave the shark a sixth sense and helped her seek prey.

o o °o

Two hours from the start of the necropsy, the tide was coming closer. Robin cut out a section of five vertebrae.

"There are rings of calcium in each vertebra. You can count the rings like a tree to find the age of the shark," she said.

"Seriously?" I asked.

"Yes," she said.

Robin sealed up the wedge-shaped section to be sent

back to the lab along with tissue samples, fish bone fragments, and a suspected tapeworm. The pups would go too.

Robin explained this was critical information. To understand and protect the white shark population, first, biologists must collect age data. If there were too many young sharks or too many old sharks in the ocean, this signaled a problem. Just like Vern Devine told us. Robin said it could be a problem with disease or reproduction. Our shark was middle-aged.

At the very end, Ray closed the flaps on the cavity and Sookie helped the biologists roll the shark into a new position. Ray sawed off the dorsal fin and said, "Poor old girl."

She looked *wrong* without the dorsal fin. The pectoral fins were removed and placed on another folding table. Our shark was a finless bullet. I thought about what Vern had said about fishermen killing sharks for their fins. After seeing the details of this shark inside and out, it seemed even more of a waste. I tried to write and draw everything I could remember in the sketch pad, so I could transfer all that Robin had explained into the field guide.

Robin invited us to touch her serrated teeth and examine her snout before Ray removed the jaws. She explained how the shark continues to make replacement teeth throughout its life.

"There's the outer row that we see," she said, sweeping her hand along the jawline. "But behind that row, there are so many spare teeth, ready to advance forward when one of the front teeth pops out. It's a continuous process."

It was like waiting in line for your name to be called.

Ray went to work on the jaws, prying them loose. "Robin told me you wanted a pair of these," he said.

"Yeah, I lost the first set," Sookie said.

It was a bloody mess that turned all of the shark's white parts pink-orange. Ray cut away at the gums and rocked the jaws from side to side like a gruesome set of false teeth until they came loose. Dad took a picture of Sookie holding the dripping jaws in the air. Without them, the shark was unrecognizable. Sookie helped the biologists carry the plastic tubs and coolers back to their trucks. Soon, the waves would carry away the remains.

"You hungry?" I asked Mr. Patterson, joking. He was sitting on a boulder, looking as though his joints might be bothering him.

"Lord, no. I think I'm going to be sick. I could have gone without that last part."

"Seriously," I said.

"What are you thinking about?" he asked.

"About the way a shark is made to do what it needs to do."

"Amazing," he said.

"Let's get Dad out of here."

Once Dad and Mr. P were safely on the sand, I trudged to where the trucks were lined up. Robin was laughing about something with Ray, while she dug through her backpack. I walked close enough to the two of them to make myself seen.

"Nice work today," Robin said to me.

"You took some copious notes," Ray said.

"Yeah," I said. "It's for a project at school."

Ray nodded. "Cool."

Robin pulled a handful of granola bars from her bag. "Anybody want one?" she asked.

I looked at her hands, wondering if it was safe for them to be touching food after where they had been. Ray took one of the bars. He thanked her, ripped open the wrapper, and started eating. Robin did the same. I guessed it was safe. Only thing was, dry oats and twigs held together by glue weren't really part of my soft foods diet.

"Lucy?" she asked, holding up the last bar.

I grabbed the snack. "Thanks."

I tore the wrapping and bit off a hunk of granola bar. *My body can do this.*

"Anybody have any water?" I asked with my mouth full.

"I have some lukewarm coffee," said Ray.

"I'll take it," I said.

Ray handed me a doll-size thermos cup, and I took small, bitter sips. It was worse than Moxie.

"When did you know that you wanted to become a marine biologist?" I asked Robin.

"When I was really young," she said. "I remember the first time I walked into the New England Aquarium. It was dark and full of concrete like a parking garage. And it smelled of fish and penguin droppings. I remember my sister pinching her nose, but not me. I liked it."

I smiled, thinking of my mom.

"Gross, I know," she said. "We walked up the ramp around the big tank in the middle. We stood at one of the observation windows and I saw the nose of a shark come into view. It was so close, I felt like I could touch it. I knew from a young age that I wanted to work outside."

Ray nodded, as though he felt the same way.

"I love the ocean," she said.

"Me too," I said. "We were going to talk about seals."

She nodded.

"When I was a grad student, I read an article that stayed with me," she said. "It predicted what might happen to the seal population off Cape Cod after the Marine Mammal Protection Act became law. Back then, seals had been my focus."

My scalp started buzzing like I knew where she was headed.

"Anyway, that article I read in school caught my eye because it talked about the next link in the chain. It talked about what was coming next, after the seals. And it was the sharks. The sharks *eat* the seals."

"So she started looking for the sharks," said Ray.

"Yup, that's when I started to focus on sharks. Do you know who wrote that article?" asked Robin.

"My mom?" I guessed.

"Your mom," she said. "I had to meet her, so I tracked her down. And I learned so many things from her."

I looked down at my granola bar and noticed it was almost gone. I had swallowed most of it. My cheeks felt hot, and my eyes stung like I was going to cry.

"Can I ask you a question?" I asked.

"Fire away."

"Do you ever swim with sharks?" I asked.

"Not on purpose," Robin said.

"My mom used to."

"I know," said Robin. "She wasn't afraid."

"Do you think that's crazy?"

"A little bit," said Robin. "But your mom always believed she was safe, and if she thought the sharks were agitated, she stayed away. Your mom wanted people to see that sharks aren't man-eaters, but I think she also wanted people to be aware that the ocean belongs to the sharks. They can breathe down there. We can't."

I nodded.

"I liked seeing the work that my mom used to do, the necropsy," I said. "Thank you."

"Anytime, Lucy," said Robin. "We are hoping to get her tags on those sharks any day now. You're welcome to come out on the boat with us."

I nodded.

I saw Mr. Patterson, Dad, and Sookie walking up slowly behind Robin. They settled into a space beside Ray.

"Thanks for your help getting the containers to the truck," Ray told Sookie.

"Thanks for the jaws," he said to both scientists.

Mr. Patterson shook hands with Ray and Robin and thanked them for the opportunity to watch the necropsy. "I never dreamed I'd see something like that today," he said.

I walked to the edge of the rocks. The waves were close to swallowing up whatever was left of the shark, the remains of muscle and organs that were already being picked apart by isopods. I watched the water wash into the cracks between the boulders, racing to see how far it could travel before being pulled back into the sea.

Dad came up beside me. He took a picture of the pile of shark in the rocks.

"Mom would have freaked out over those shark pups. I can see her face," Dad said as he looked at me.

"Didn't she see a lot of those?" I asked, thinking of the woman in the Cousteau book, looking at the babies pouring out of the mother shark.

"Not white shark pups," said Dad. "Remember what Vern said? Your mom was looking for a range of different ages. A healthy community has young sharks, middle-aged sharks, and old sharks."

"Except the community just lost two young sharks," I said.

"That's true," Dad said. "But it means there are probably more out there."

Mr. Patterson stood next to me, and Sookie pulled up beside Dad. We watched a wave crash onto the rocks, dragging part of the shark out with it. I wondered how long it would take for there to be no trace of the shark. For the rocks to be clean, for the creatures in the ocean to eat the rest of it, for a three-thousand-pound shark to dissolve.

"That's all she wrote," Mr. Patterson said, as we watched a section of the tail sink into the water.

"You wanna head back?" Dad asked.

"Yeah, I'm starving," Sookie said. "What's for lunch?"

"Good Lord, you're hungry after that?" Mr. Patterson said.

"We could pick up something on the way home," Dad said.

"I guess I could eat," Mr. Patterson said.

We walked up the beach, with Dad on one crutch. I held on to his other arm.

33. *The Field Guide*

MS. SOLOMON GREW VEGETABLES IN HER FRONT YARD. THERE were huge wooden beds, a jungle of leaves, and ripe crops right under the dining room window. I walked between the rows of beans, climbing up a twine grid, and the low, bushy vines spilling squash across the plot. It smelled like tomatoes and dirt. I could hear a bee buzzing nearby, and I tugged on the straps of my backpack, hurrying up the porch steps.

I knocked on the glass pane of her old front door and waited.

Ms. Solomon opened the door with a baby on her hip. Rosie. I had seen her in the school a bunch of times last year and heard about her much more frequently in Ms. Solomon's science class. I already knew Rosie didn't sleep well, that she liked avocados, and that she was named for Ms. Solomon's grandmother. Today, the baby was gumming a washcloth.

"Lucy," said Ms. Solomon, smiling. "What're you doing here?"

"I was hoping you'd be around," I said. "Hi, Rosie."

Rosie stared at me with huge, bulging eyes like a younger Vern Devine. She kept gnawing on the cloth and looking at my face.

"Is it an okay time?" I asked.

"Of course. Come in," said Ms. Solomon.

We walked into the house and down the hall, Rosie watching me over her mother's shoulder. I smiled at her, but she looked at me like I was someone to be avoided.

"Come into the kitchen," said Ms. Solomon.

She plunked Rosie in a wooden highchair and put some blueberries on the tray. Rosie pinched a berry with her fingers and rolled it between her lips, shivering at the tart taste. All this time, she kept her eyes on me.

"She likes you," said Ms. Solomon.

"Could have fooled me," I said.

"She's curious. She's trying to figure you out."

I shrugged and pulled my backpack around to the front. "I have something to show you."

I unzipped the bag and pulled out the blue canvas journal, placing it on the kitchen table.

Ms. Solomon picked up the book, brought it to the head of the table, and sat down. I stood behind Ms. Solomon, near Rosie, who had popped another blueberry into her mouth. Ms. Solomon opened the cover and looked down at the title page, nodding.

"It's the field guide," she said, looking up at me. "Can I take a look?"

"Yeah, that's why I'm here," I said.

She nodded and turned to the book. I thought maybe she would scan the pages, but ask to keep it, so she could read it more thoroughly later. She was reading every word.

"That's the merganser we found at Mill Pond," I said, pointing to the duck with a Mohawk. "The day Fred and I spotted it, I lost my sneaker in the marsh, trying to get close."

"Good effort," she said.

"We had one rule," I said. "We only could include the animal if we saw it with our own eyes. So it's not really a complete guide to Cape Ann."

She peeked ahead to the last page in the book we'd filled, about halfway through the journal. "I'd say you saw quite a bit."

"Fred wrote most of the text and I made all the illustrations," I said.

"Very nice markings, Lucy," she said.

"Thanks."

Ms. Solomon was a terrible artist, but she always encouraged us to draw. Her sketches on the chalkboard looked like preschool illustrations that someone had poked a hole in and deflated. It always perked me up when she drew in class.

She read the pages about the sea urchin, the horseshoe crab, and the moon snail. At which point, Rosie let out a huge squawk, like a crow. Without looking up from the guide, Ms. Solomon said, "Lucy, can you grab the box of Cheerios on the counter and give some to Rosie."

"Uh, okay," I said.

I looked at Rosie. Rosie looked at me as I put a handful of Cheerios onto her tray. She wiggled both wrists like she was turning two doorknobs, excited. I sat down at the table.

"I love that you included the golden ratio and the shells on the beach with the holes in them," Ms. Solomon said about the moon snail. "Beautiful color and dimension, Lucy."

"Thanks," I said.

Now, I could see Ms. Solomon's face. She was very quiet, though she nodded a couple of times. It was an extra-credit project, so I wasn't going to flunk science if she didn't like the field guide. But I felt jittery, wondering what she was thinking. I don't ever remember caring about a project as much before, or working so hard. I kept waiting for her to come to the last section, to the part about the white sharks. After the Cheerios and another handful of berries for Rosie, Ms. Solomon made it to the white shark page.

Even though Fred and I started the research together, the white shark page was blank when he died. I entered all of the text and the drawings myself. I took his words and ran with them. The section was at least five times longer than any of the other ones. Fred probably would have disagreed with this. It might have implied that white sharks were more important than mergansers or spotted salamanders, but to me they were.

Ms. Solomon picked up the washcloth that Rosie had

been chewing, and Rosie followed the cloth to her mother's face. The baby watched silently as her mom wiped her eyes.

"Well done, Lucy," she said. "When you're a teacher, you always hope that your student will find something meaningful in the assignment to latch on to and that she'll make it her own."

"For most of the project, I think I was along for the ride, helping Fred," I confessed.

"When did it become yours?" she asked. "When the shark got stuck in the net?"

I shook my head. "Not exactly. I think it was seeing my mom on TV that night. It made me curious."

Ms. Solomon nodded.

"Every time I tried to draw the shark it looked like a blob, or a windup toy. So I started trying to fix it."

"Sharks stay in constant motion. It's hard to capture that," she said.

"Yeah," I said. "I started looking at all of the different parts and how they work. And I drew and drew and drew."

"I knew you would catch things that Fred wouldn't see," she said. "But artists and scientists aren't really that different, you know. They both want to figure out how things work."

I remembered gutting fish with Sookie the day we talked about why Mom liked dissecting things.

"Why does a squid have three hearts?" I said.

"I think they have two hearts that feed the gills and one

larger heart that pumps blood to the rest of the squid. They need high levels of oxygen in their blood to survive."

"But why?" I asked.

"Well," she said. "Squid have two lines of defense: squirting ink and escaping quickly. They need a lot of oxygen to move away from predators. Maybe they have three hearts to keep up the oxygen supply."

I looked at the drawings of the shark teeth, the rows and rows, just waiting in line to pop forward.

"Kind of amazing how animals are built to survive," I said.

"Yes. They adapt."

Rosie made a humming noise, so I looked over. She put a blueberry to her lips, still watching me, unsure. Then she pulled it away and reached the berry up to my face. She fed me with her slimy fingers. I gave the berry a good mash and swallowed it with no trouble.

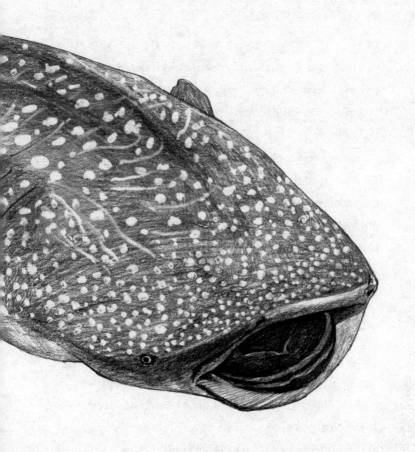

34. *Darkroom*

IN FRONT OF THE OPEN REFRIGERATOR, I UNWRAPPED A piece of leftover pizza and took a quick bite, like a shark, trying to decide if it was really worth eating. Nope.

I closed the fridge and spotted a bowl of peaches on the counter. The smell of the ripe fruit was so strong that I could almost taste it before I got my lips around it. My teeth snapped the fuzzy skin and I wiped the juice from the corner of my mouth. This was one of the last great summer peaches. After I swallowed, I heard a noise coming from below the kitchen floor, like metal scraping concrete.

I opened the cellar door. "Dad?"

"Down here," he yelled.

I walked down the steep staircase, wondering how he made it to the bottom in his cast. We had a real basement. Dirty, cement floor, wires and pipes, and terrible lighting, but at least I couldn't see the cobwebs or ghosts who'd probably been hanging around since Lincoln was president.

When I got to the bottom, I smelled the darkroom— chemicals, vinegar, and something sweet. I knew it was safe to go inside when I saw the light coming from behind the cracked door. I took a bite of the peach, slurping back the juice.

I pushed the door open quietly. Dad stood over the trays with his weight on both feet, against doctor's rules. He transferred prints from a tray of chemicals to the water bath in the last container and gently swished them with a pair of tongs.

I looked to the left where he had hung a series of prints on a clothesline over the long, old work sink. Dad clipped a dripping photo on the line.

"Whoa," I said, startling Dad.

He looked over his shoulder. "It took me all summer to finish a roll of film."

I took a noisy bite and looked at his work.

"Don't eat in here. Throw that out," he said, pointing at the peach like it was contaminated.

I couldn't believe he was telling me to stop eating. "Fine."

On one side of the clothesline was the beginning of the summer. I stared at a picture of Fred and Mr. Patterson.

"When did you take that one?" I asked, pointing.

"Fourth of July. They were out on Ernie's porch, playing their instruments."

Mr. P was blowing into the French horn, and Fred was watching him, his trumpet in his hands.

"I'm really sorry that we're not going to get a chance to see where that kid was headed," Dad said.

"Me too."

I looked up at the half smile on Fred's face, wondering

whether he still had liked playing patriotic songs with Mr. P, while he was listening to experimental jazz upstairs in his room. I got chills on the back of my neck, like Fred was tapping his toe on my foot.

There were photos of Sookie's shark, bound and hanging in a loop on the wharf, the heads of people in the crowd framing the huge fish.

"I forgot you took pictures that day," I said.

We looked up at the photo of Fred and me in front of Sookie's shark. Even in black-and-white, my face seemed red. Fred's curls were dark around his hairline from sweat.

"I was a lot taller than him," I said.

"You were."

There was a photo of Sookie talking to Lester under the shark.

"I thought I'd give that one to Sook."

I nodded. "I was mad at you that day."

"For what?" he said.

"For going diving at the beach. I didn't want you to be eaten by a shark. Then I'd have no parents," I said.

"Lucy."

"No, I don't want to hear the statistics or probability or whatever. That's just how I felt."

Dad looked at the shark photos. "I needed to clear my head," he said. "When Sookie caught the shark, I thought, 'She should have been here. She missed it.'"

"I know," I said.

There were photos of the dive team, taken on the banks of Salem Harbor. Most of the divers just looked like insects, indistinguishable in their masks and regulators, but there was one shot that felt human. It was a photo of a guy in a life vest and baseball cap with one hand on a diver's back and a bag of rope in the other. Dad stared at it for a few seconds.

"The line tender." I recognized him from the quarry.

"Uh-huh," he said.

"Do you miss them?" I said. "The team?"

He nodded.

I walked farther down the line to the photos from the necropsy, the shark twisted into the rocks like a huge white sea monster washed up from the pages of an old story. Some of the photos were gruesome, but there was a closeup of the intestines that seemed like a photo of a beautiful sculpture.

"That's my favorite one," Dad said, moving to the last photo, the one he'd been hanging when I walked in the room.

It was me, crouched beside the carcass, drawing on my sketch pad. Just me and a big dead shark.

"Did you ever think you'd be *there*?" he asked.

"Not without Fred. Or Mom," I said. "Why's it your favorite?"

"It reminds me of them," he said. "But it also reminds me of you. You're determined to figure out that shark. And you're sensitive to the details."

"Plus, I look pretty tough."

"Definitely," he said. "You'd make a good line tender."

"'Cause I avoid the water?" I asked, not even joking.

"No. The line tender sees *everything*. Reads the divers' signals, the terrain, the equipment. Uses all the resources to stay connected to the other end of the line."

"Who's on the other end?" I asked. "Mom? Fred? I'm pretty sure I lost them."

"You didn't," he said. "Look."

He pointed again to his favorite photo.

"Part of it is them. And part of it is you. Some lines don't break."

35. *As Fluid as the Fish*

MY ROOM HAD BECOME A DUMP. MOST OF MY CLOTHING WAS on the floor in dirty heaps. My drawers were so empty, I was wearing an old soccer uniform. Dad had stopped by a couple of times in the last week to collect dirty clothes, but I didn't want to deal with it, so I sent him away.

And it wasn't only clothes. There were half-empty teacups that were now homes to bacterial colonies. My wastebasket was overflowing with crumpled drawing paper and pencil shavings. Just about everything I had touched this summer hadn't been returned to its origin. It was all here.

There was a knock at the door.

"I'm cleaning," I said.

"The prints are dry," Dad said from the hallway. "Do you have room for them, or should I hang on to 'em?"

I opened the door. "I'll make room."

Dad went back downstairs and I carried his photos over to my desk. I pinned the photo of Fred and me under Sookie's shark to the bulletin board, next to the photo of Mom, Dad, and Sookie when they were young. I rearranged a few things to make room for Dad's favorite picture, the one of me crouching next to the shark with my sketch pad.

If I was ready to clean up, I knew that I should start

with one thing. Just start somewhere. Ms. Solomon asked to keep the field guide, so she could write up comments for me. With the project finished, I decided to reshelve the books that Fred and I had borrowed from Mom's library. They were all over the place—on my desk, in a pile beside my bed with a glass of old water on top, and under the windowsill. I gathered them and carried them into Mom's office, stacking them in front of the bookshelf. I tried to remember what went where, knowing that with Fred and Mom gone, nobody was going to notice if the books were in the wrong places.

I reached up to place the book by Cousteau and Cousteau in a gap on the high shelf and saw a black box that had a little metal placard, like an empty placeholder for a name tag.

"What's in this one?' I asked, pulling down the box. It had a lid and was the size of a shoebox for kids with wide feet. I removed the lid of the nameless box. Videotapes.

I brought them down to the rug and pulled each one out of the box. The last three read:

> Basking shark necropsy
> WHOI lecture series
> Nature documentary

For some reason, the one marked "Nature documentary" made my scalp buzz. I stood up and fed the tape into the TV/VCR combo in the corner. The screen was covered in dust, like a light snowfall, and I wiped the glass clear with my shirt.

The tape began in the middle of an interview with Mom. I recognized it immediately. There she was with her hair blowing softly around her face and her shoulders moving with the gentle sway of the boat. It was the same TV footage that Fred and I watched the day that Sookie had hauled the white shark into Rockport.

"Holy fish," I whispered, with a rock in my gut.

"Am I afraid? Being in the water with sharks?" Mom grinned. "No. You just have to remember that you are swimming in their home. You have to know how to behave when you are the guest."

I didn't remember her ever filming this, but then again, when she was here, I never had paid much attention to what she did when she wasn't with me.

But I was fixated now.

"There is so much we *don't* know about them," she said. "Where they go and why, or how many there are? What do their behaviors mean? And people fear what they don't know. If we knew more about sharks, maybe we would be in a better position to help ensure their survival."

The census.

And then there was the moment where she had smiled at me before and I had dropped the phone. This time I held her gaze.

"But aren't you afraid?" the interviewer asked her. "Do you have children?"

"You wouldn't ask a man that question," she said calmly.

It was silent for a moment before the interviewer said, "Fair enough."

But she answered anyway. "I have a daughter," she said in a voice as warm as light in a greenhouse. "I am always thinking of my daughter and the line of generations that will follow her. Humans have a great impact on the ocean. There is still time to reverse what we've done."

I have a daughter. I am always thinking of my daughter. Lately, I had been wondering if she had been thinking about me when she got in the water with sharks. Had it been worth putting her life in danger to understand shark behavior or to try to prove to people that sharks aren't man-eaters? I still thought she might have been a little crazy.

The next thing I knew, the camera people were filming her in scuba gear, flipping backward off the side of the boat. It took two tries for me to swallow. It was her own body, and not the sharks, which would eventually kill her. But when the camera below the surface captured footage of her plunging into the water, I stopped thinking about dark things. She looked like a dolphin, being born into the water, swimming away just seconds after birth. Swimming underwater, my mom was graceful and at ease.

I paused the tape.

"Dad! Sookie!" I cried.

At an unimpressive speed, Sookie appeared in the doorway, followed by my dad.

"What?" said Sookie.

"You've gotta see this," I said, rewinding the tape back to the beginning of the section. His expression changed.

"That's what we saw on TV!" Sookie said.

Dad just watched.

She swam alongside the rope that was anchored to the bottom and into a shipwreck, covered in earthy greens. There were little fish of various sizes swimming around everywhere and then the sharks came into focus. They swam by my mom like a fleet of small ships moving through the wreck, their sandy-brown skin gliding past her, caudal fins rippling like fabric through the water.

I was surprised by the way the sharks swam at a slow pace and how they seemed to pay no attention to her at all. They must have known she was there, but maybe she knew just how to blend in. She didn't reach out to touch them. She swam parallel to the sharks, just another creature in the ocean.

"I remember this," Dad said. "Where did you find the tape?"

He was clearly distracted because there was a pile of VHS tapes on the floor next to the box.

"In the bookshelf," I said.

I stopped paying attention to the TV and observed Sookie and Dad as they watched Mom, her black form keeping pace with the brown sharks, sailing through an exit in the shipwreck, as fluid as the fish. Dad leaned a little deeper into his crutch. Sookie put his hands on his hips. It was like she had knocked them both a little off balance.

When the narrator abruptly cut to footage of whale sharks in Saudi Arabia, far away from Mom's ocean, Dad said, "Play it again."

It was a little strange to me that Sookie and Dad had both loved my mom (and they were okay with it), but watching her navigate a strange world so capably made us all want to truly understand how she worked. She was kind of amazing.

The third time through the clip, there was a knock on the doorframe. It was Fiona.

"No one answered. I let myself in," she said.

I waved her over.

Fiona stood in front of the TV, eyeing the sharks that sailed past the diver.

"What are we watching?" she asked.

"Mom," I said.

Fiona looked at me. Then she stared at the screen.

A sand shark passed over Mom's head, swimming through the bubbles rising from her regulator. The camera tracked Mom as she followed the shark, as though she were flying by us. Her flippers rippled and she was gone.

"Real women look like *that*," I said.

Fiona put her arm around me.

We watched the clip one more time before Sookie and Dad headed back downstairs to see the baseball game, but on his way out the door, Sookie turned to me and said, "I called Robin after the necropsy."

"Really?" I said.

He nodded. "I told her I'd help them tag the sharks."

I smiled.

"I told Robin I'd try to get you to come with me," he said.

I looked at Fiona. "I'll go."

o o o o

That night, I dreamed about the quarry. I was below the surface. The water was dull green, like the trees in a Hudson River School painting, but it looked glassy and clear. While I was treading water and breathing like a mermaid, a white shark swam closer, the side-to-side movement of his tail propelling the shark forward. Like I had X-ray goggles, I could see each vertebra shift as he glided around me. I turned to watch the shark, as nervous as a kid might feel waiting for her name to be called for a doctor's checkup, but nothing more. I labeled his fins in my mind, the quarry water flowing through his gills. He drew another loop around me before swimming away, and as he sailed by, he made a *ping*.

36. *Ping*

DAD ONCE TOLD ME TO LOOK AT THE HORIZON TO KEEP from getting seasick, but it was impossible to get a fix on it while holed up in the cabin of a harpoon boat that had windows the size of Kleenex boxes.

Mr. Patterson slowly came down the steps into the dark cabin for the second time. He was wearing a white sun hat and huge, dark glasses that reminded me of Fred.

"Any sharks?" I asked.

"Not yet," he said. "But you're not going to see any down here. You should come up."

"I will," I said.

He wasn't moving.

"This was your idea," he said, looking me in the eye.

"I know."

I wanted to get out there, but I still felt shaky on the water.

I followed him up the stairs, the waves rocking the boat up and down. I took careful steps toward the bow of the boat, to see what Sookie was up to. My heart nearly stopped when I saw him at the far edge of the narrow catwalk, nearly a boat's length away, dangling over the ocean like bait at the end of a fishing pole. Sookie stood in a waist-high, metal pulpit, with his back to us, holding on to a long metal stick. A harpoon with an acoustic tag.

He seemed so far away from us, from the boat, in a tiny cage. I wondered what it felt like to be hovering like that with only a thin railing between him and the water, when I could barely keep my balance on the boat. Sookie looked more steady than the rest of us.

"I'm going to go sit with your father," Mr. Patterson said, working his way across the deck.

I sucked in a big breath, connecting the parts of the scene. There was a spotter plane, looking for sharks from above. Sookie hung over the ocean, yards beyond the boat with the harpoon in hand, waiting for the white shark to swim underneath him, so he could tag the fish. It was as if the drawings in Mom's proposal had come to life.

It felt cool on the boat, even though it had been another warm August day, so I wore a thick sweatshirt. A pair of binoculars hung from my neck, swinging back and forth as I tacked around the deck, moving from one stationary object I could grab to the next, like I was learning to walk again.

My head felt dizzy, maybe because of the rocking motion of the boat or the hum of the engine. I held on to the metal rail along the side of the boat, looking out into the water. There were small waves inside the big waves, and the surface reminded me of an elephant's wrinkled skin with lines in all directions. I watched the peaks and valleys of the big waves, waiting for something large to be revealed in the ups and downs, like a whale or a shark.

The pilot's voice came over the boat's radio in a fog of static. It reminded me of Mr. Patterson's police scanner.

"*Bfff* . . . He's turning right now. He's turning right," the pilot said.

I gripped the railing and looked at Robin on deck. "What's turning right?" I yelled to her.

"A shark," she said. "A white."

Robin was standing at the beginning of the catwalk, smiling, shouting at Sookie. The team had been out on the boat several times in the past week, but managed to successfully tag only one white shark. If they wanted to collect enough data for their study, they would need several more. The shark turning right was Number Two.

"Right there," Sookie yelled.

It was as if the shark had sensed it was being watched, stalked even, because right when Sookie aimed the harpoon at the fish, the shark shifted in a different direction.

"*Bfff* . . . He's turning," said the pilot between farty blips.

"Get him! Get him!" Robin yelled.

But it was too late. Sookie had released the harpoon into the water like an arrow that sailed far beyond the outermost circle of a target. Missed. Even the clams that were tucked away in the muck could hear him curse.

Robin walked slowly out to the pulpit with a second harpoon, stopping after the first couple of steps to get her balance and maybe find the nerve to keep going. Over my shoulder, I spotted a third harpoon leaning several yards away from the catwalk, loaded with another acoustic tag. I thought about picking it up and waiting near the edge of the catwalk, in case Sookie needed it.

The radio crackled. "He's going for the starboard side."

That's my side.

My heart started beating faster. Without thinking I grabbed the harpoon in the middle like I was a javelin thrower. But I didn't walk it to Sookie. I turned to face the waves off the starboard side of the boat. I climbed up on the ledge and leaned my stomach against the metal rail, watching the water in the space between Sookie's catwalk and me. I was like Fred shucking off his sweatshirt at the quarry, running to the edge of the cliff.

"*Bfff* . . . Uh-oh. The kid is taking aim. Somebody move," the spotter pilot said in a monotone voice over the radio, as though it were no big deal that I was about to launch an acoustic tracking device onto the seafloor.

"I got this one!" I yelled out.

I heard people's sneakers slapping the deck in an anxious attempt to stop me, but I knew I could do it. I knew this shark as well as any of the adults on the boat. I had drawn its body inside and out—the vertebrae like cartilaginous Legos, the placement of the organs, the fins, and the industrial hinges of the jaw. I knew this shark. I scrubbed one hundred attempts clean with my eraser, trying to get the right distance between the fins or the right amount of muscular girth. And each time I messed up, I was one step closer to understanding how fast this creature moved, how those jaws could pop out like a lizard throwing its tongue to catch a fly.

So, with people yelling my name, I saw the shark's shadow coming into view just below the surface. And I threw the heavy javelin like a warrior, ahead of where I wanted it to land: in that fleshy part, right below the dorsal fin.

"*Bfff* . . . She got it!" the spotter pilot yelled, his voice cracking. "Shark's about fourteen feet long."

I watched the shark wiggle, like he was trying to scratch an itch on his back, and I ran along the railing to get ahead of him, so I could see him swim by. I held on to the railing and leaned over to look, my hair whipping my cheeks. The long body glided by with the power of one hundred Olympic swimmers, seemingly with zero effort. His skin looked brown just under the surface, unlike the slate-gray color of Sookie's shark that hung on the dock, or the one that washed up on the Cape. I wanted to reach out and touch its back, which was covered in denticles, V-shaped scales that were like teeth all over the shark's body. The denticles decreased drag and made the shark able to swim quickly and quietly. I wondered what they felt like gliding through the water.

"Holy fish," I whispered, as I watched the fin and tail sink below the surface and slip away. The shark descended until it was out of sight. There was a breeze in my face. I imagined it was the tailwinds of the shark and I breathed in.

When I turned around, Robin, Dad, Mr. Patterson, and Sookie were all looking at me. I couldn't believe what I'd done either.

Dad grabbed my elbow and leaned over to look me in the eye. "Lucy Elizabeth Everhart. That was important equipment that many scientists—including your mother—worked hard to get. It's not yours to pitch off the boat!"

"I'm sorry, Dad," I said. "I wasn't thinking."

"No, you weren't," he said.

I looked at Robin. She seemed both angry and stunned. And maybe worried, like she might have invited some kind of a delinquent onto the boat.

"Lucy," she said, breathing heavy and talking slowly. "I do appreciate that you tagged that shark. In fact, it's kind of a miracle. But I would prefer if you left the job to Sookie from here on. Okay?"

I nodded. "Sure thing," I said. "I'm sorry."

"I'm gonna check on Ray and see if he's got anything on the receiver," she said. Robin hesitated for a second, then she turned to me. "My mother used to tell me that the best defense for anything is doing a good job."

She lowered her chin and looked me straight in the eye.

I stared back. Robin walked over to the equipment.

Sookie shook his head.

"What?" I asked.

"I can't believe I whiffed and you nailed it," he said. "You gotta admit, Tom. It was pretty impressive."

Dad sat down on the ledge, leaned his crutch against the rail, and sighed.

Mr. Patterson lowered himself beside Dad. "Sookie's right."

Robin was talking to the spotter pilot over the radio, and Ray was listening on the headphones to see if he could pick up the shark's ping. I walked over to Ray and pulled up the hood on my sweatshirt.

"Can you hear it?" I asked.

Ray nodded, but he looked unsure and adjusted a knob on the receiver. With his other hand, he turned a handle that was attached to a pipe, running down the side of the boat, into the water. At the bottom of the pipe was the hydrophone, a piece of equipment that could pick up the shark's ping from the tag. The ping was strongest when the hydrophone was pointing directly at the tag.

"Do you have him?" Robin yelled to Ray.

Ray nodded. "Yup."

Ray pulled the headphones off his ears and let them dangle around his neck. "We're gonna let you name this one," he said. "Since you tagged it."

"Thanks. Its name is Fred. What does it sound like?" I asked Ray.

"The ping?"

"Yeah."

"You want to listen?" he asked.

I nodded. He put the enormous headphones over my ears. I adjusted the headband. At first, we heard fuzz, static like on Mr. Patterson's police scanner. I shook my head at Ray. But then there was a sound. It was like my elementary music teacher, banging on a handheld wood block with a little mallet. *Bom, bom, bom.* Then static for a few beats, like a rest in a piece of music. *Bom, bom, bom.*

Fred the Shark was making a pattern, slightly irregular, like a kid learning to play an instrument. *Bom, bom, bom.* I closed my eyes and listened to a long stretch of fuzz. *Bom, bom, bom.*

It could have been straight out of Fred's Miles Davis album, where the musicians made sounds that had never been made by instruments before. But for some reason, when Fred the Shark played the notes, I wanted to keep listening. It reminded me of what Mr. Patterson had said on our way back from Maine. *Maybe you have to see it performed live to appreciate it. Keep your mind open to it.*

In the static rests, I started echoing the pings in my head. After Fred the Shark said, *Bom, bom, bom*, I said, *Bom, bom, bom*, and he would respond again. It went on that way for a minute or two. Then I started filling the rests with thoughts, things I would have written to Fred in a postcard.

"I just saw a great white swim by."

Bom, bom, bom.

"Ray thinks I am hogging the headphones."

Bom, bom, bom.

"The shark is named Fred. You're a shark."

Bom, bom, bom.

Ray tapped me on the shoulder, and I opened my eyes. He raised his eyebrows, pointed to the headphones, and then he poked himself in the sternum. I didn't want to give them away, so I held up a finger, as if to tell him I needed one more minute. *Bom, bom, bom.*

I didn't know whether Fred the Shark was ten meters below us, or one hundred meters to the west. There was an art to interpreting the pings that even Ray and Robin hadn't learned yet. No one on the boat knew how far away or how deep he was. I leaned over, hoping to catch a glimpse of the fins coming to the surface. In the North Atlantic, the waves were dark and opaque, but I still looked over the side of the boat, trying to see deeper.

Ray looked at me, and I made a puzzled expression.

"Something happened," I said. "Everything just changed."

I handed him the headphones. I watched him listen until his eyes grew wide.

"I think we're listening to two different pings," he yelled. "I think it's Helen."

I looked at him, confused.

"The first shark," he said. "We named her Helen."

"She's here?" I asked.

Ray nodded.

"Robin, come listen to this," Ray called, but she didn't

hear him. She was talking to Sookie at the edge of the cat-walk. "Here. Hold these."

Ray handed me the headphones and moved toward the prow of the boat, steadying himself against the corner of the wheelhouse. I tried to separate the two pings. The rhythm had shifted. The rests were shorter between pings and there was a new sound, *Bom, bom, bee, bee, bom, bee.* It was dissonant and chaotic. I cupped my hands over the tan plastic ear muffs and said out loud, "It's Mom."

I had read somewhere that white sharks were solitary creatures, crossing great distances alone, but that some-times they swam in pairs. No one knows why they do this. Somewhere near the boat, Helen and Fred were swimming together. I listened to the strange music they made, like it was an old, favorite song. I imagined them cruising around Monomoy Island, talking to each other. Maybe Helen had been pinging for a long time, waiting for one of us to join her below the waves.

ACKNOWLEDGMENTS

I AM DEEPLY GRATEFUL TO MY AGENT, MICHAEL BOURRET, for believing in the story and guiding me through the process of publishing this book.

Many thanks to the team at Dutton and Penguin Young Readers Group, especially Julie Strauss-Gabel, Melissa Faulner, Natalie Vielkind, Jessica Jenkins, Lindsey Andrews, Rosanne Lauer, Anne Heausler, and my editor, Andrew Karre, for knowing how to balance the story, reducing noise in some places and raising the volume in others. To Xingye Jin, who created a powerful cover and captured the essential lines of Lucy's drawings. Thank you all for bringing this book to life.

I'd like to thank the experts, for sharing their deep knowledge and being gracious with their time: Greg Skomal, Brad Chase, Lieutenant William Freeman, Captain Conrad Prosniewski, Al Drinkwater, Mike Birarelli, Tom Bartlett, Sooky Sawyer, Tracey Steig, and Michael Kinzer. Any inaccuracies are my fault, not theirs. There were several people whose work inspired and moved me along like a current throughout the writing process: Eugenie Clark, Alexa Canady, Joy Reidenberg, Jane Goodall, Jacques Cousteau, Rachel Carson, Susan Allen, and Ashanti Johnson.

I can't imagine writing a book without Supergroup: Jana Hiller, Kaethe Schwehn, Sarah Hanley, Sean Beggs, Coralee Grebe, Brian Rubin, Kristi Belcamino, and Christy Kujawa, who read this story again and again, providing honest feedback, humor, and support. And thank you to the Loft for connecting me with these people, and for providing classes and a community for writers in the Twin Cities.

Many thanks to my writing mentors, especially Charlotte Gordon, who helped me find my voice and loaded my high school writing class into a van to see Adrienne Rich read her poems. And Mary Gardner, who told me she'd shoot herself if this book didn't get published (as she kindly reminded me that the manuscript wasn't going to query itself). Also, Rob Farnsworth and Gary Lawless for suggesting that I make something out of that poem about the scuba diver. And David Housewright for insisting that fiction writers do their research.

Cincy Schradle, Kate Owens, Paul Legler, Lisa Li, and Christine Brunkhorst were the early readers who encouraged me to keep going.

I'm grateful for the support of my dear friends, Cecily Cullinan, Zoe Adler, and Kate O'Brien; and my beloved colleagues on the proposal team: Eric Chalmers, John Nelson, Jennifer Winsten, Karla Snellings, Amy Johnson, Caitlin Stollenwerk, Julie Jenkins, (and Alicia DeGross).

I owe a great deal of thanks to my family. Barbara and Dan Schultz, and Marilyn Vinokour, took care of my children (on winter nights in Minnesota), so I could make it to writing class or Supergroup. They also introduced me to the Loft. My aunt, Pamela Parrella, is one of the first writers I ever knew and I've been grateful to share updates with her throughout the years. Many thanks to my cousin, Alex Penfold, for her advice.

I owe just about everything to my parents. My mother remembers summer vacations at the Cape and my father shared the waters with sharks in his tiny boat when he was Lucy's age. They passed on their love of the ocean to me, which is the heart of this story, but they inspire me in countless other ways. I'd also like to thank Cynthia Allen, one of the best teachers on earth, and Dave Deinstadt, my research partner.

Many thanks to my boys, Sam and Leo, who helped me write to the end of the story, so that we could keep reading the manuscript together. They make everything better.

I'm deeply grateful to Jon, for our years in Rockport (and everywhere else) and for always being my partner in crime. He helped me believe I was a writer, even when I had nothing to show for it.